IN A TIME OF MAGIC
Arnold W. Porter

To those who returned to the land
and their children
who sprang forth from it.

I
Last Snow

Ryan arose early, not bothering to start a fire. He heard the first car of the day come down Main Road and threw on his sweater and coat. He grabbed his broad brimmed cowboy hat and flung the pack that he had filled the night before over his shoulder. He ran out the door. Too late for that ride.

Up at the corner, he stood on the road in front of the empty school bus shelter, a shack built of shakes and poles with a bench inside for the kids to sit. He moved to stay warm and listened for the sound of another car coming through the forest. After awhile he heard the rise and fall of its exhaust as it navigated the peaks and valleys of Main Road.

Island cars were not that great to begin with, two hundred dollar wonders, but at least, in their former lifetimes, they had been pasted together to keep them legally on the road. Here, with no car ferry, they ran outside the law and were hidden in the bush whenever the RCMP came over. On the dirt roads fenders, mufflers, even doors, fell off and lay by the side of the road. Ryan sometimes thought of island cars as musical instruments, their unmuffled exhausts belching deep resonances into the silent forest, their loose parts flapping and clanking in percussive accompaniment. Sometimes he could identify who was coming by the sound alone. As the vehicle got closer he could tell that it was a truck by its widely rattling fenders.

Finally, an old International Harvester came out through the tunnel of trees and stopped for Ryan. He waved to the people in the cab and then climbed into the back with the other passengers. Everyone was huddled as close to the cab as they could get, wrapped in coats and scarves, heads down out of the wind. They looked up briefly and waved at him with gloved hands before returning to their huddling.

It was too cold to talk, so they wound along in windy, rattling silence, past the lake where the drowned trees stood like ghosts in the misty waters, past the old bootlegger's house with its coffee and teapot shaped chimneys, past the long arm of Mud Bay where they got their first look at the sea. Everyone looked up. There were no waves breaking on the rocky little islets out past the mouth of the bay. It would be a flat-calm crossing.

As the truck slowly crunched its way down the steep road to the wharf, spitting rocks from under its tires, they all turned to see who was sitting in the warm cafe drinking coffee. Then they rolled out onto the planks of the pier, the truck pressing tire marks into fingers of hoarfrost that looked like they were reaching up to pull them back into winter.

The sea was flat and grey. The sky hung like a defeated army's banner. Everyone carried their bundles down the ramp to where the ferry floated peacefully tied to the dock. Blisters of rust oozed out from under its gummy green paint. Rumour had it that if you put your ear to the hull, you could hear the rust working away inside like termites.

A motley collection of cars and trucks began to descend to the wharf. The new deckhand came on his bicycle and climbed aboard the ferry. After some clanking below deck, the ferry's engine roared into life. The drivers unloaded their vehicles and drove them back up the hill to hide them in the trees by the Abandoned Church.

Since safety regulations required that the boat, an old logging crummy, could carry no more than 21 passengers, the deckhand gave out boarding passes to the people who were already waiting and to others as they arrived. In reality, the "boarding passes" were 21

3

playing cards that the deckhand carried in his back pocket. The new deckhand, the first of the newtimers to hold the job, had substituted Major Arcana from the Tarot for the normal playing cards. Ryan wondered if he was playing with a full deck himself.

Friday was a popular shopping day, and Ryan had come early to be sure to get on the ferry. Yet, deeply superstitious, he held back from taking a Tarot card. What if he got Death or the Tower? Should he cancel his desperately needed trip and condemn himself to more isolation and silent time trapped in his own head? Suddenly the deckhand was in front of him, curly black hair springing out from under his Cowichan toque. "OK Ryan, time to choose!" He held out the remaining cards in a face-down fan and nodded at Ryan, a devilish grin on his face. Unable to take another week on the island, Ryan picked a card, deciding that he would go regardless of the consequences. He was relieved as he turned it over and saw that it was The World, with a picture of a naked Goddess floating in the air. The deckhand said "cool man" and nodded significantly. Ryan's mood changed instantly. His face lit up in a smile. The card put a good light on his trip, promised a good time off the island and even the possibility of a romantic adventure.

It seemed to him that in his twenty three years, he had already been flung from The Tower. Since moving to the island, his marriage had ended, his wife and daughter had left the country, and his island car didn't run. He felt like a character from a country and western song. Depression, relieved only by the transitory euphoria of drugs, had settled in. He looked around the dock at his fellow islanders and saw too much change marked on each of their faces. They spoke of "going through changes," as though it was a normal event like cutting wood, having a birthday, or getting the flu.

A popular notion, borrowed perhaps from Buddhism or Avaita—no one was too sure about the source of things—was that they were going through many lifetimes in one body: in simpler times you lived a life and died; not much happened. Then you were born again, lived another life, learned a few more lessons, grew a bit, and died. Not much happened. Now it felt like lifetimes were hatching in each person like mayflies: people left marriages, professions; started new ones; ended them, moved on; started over only to end again. Each person suffered many births and deaths, many families, many jobs, many towns. Perhaps it was the bomb that their parents had left so considerately hanging over their heads, the feeling of doom, that created all this frantic trying on of costumes. But now the changing room was a mess and the sales lady was getting grumpy. As The Poet sang, *There Must Be Some Way Out of Here*. They had all come here to recreate Eden out among the fruit trees planted by a previous generation. All the hard work, the clearing, the building of log houses had already been done. They were like the angelic grandchildren, shot through with light and drugs, escaping the cities, returning to the land. They felt blessed to have escaped the corruption of civilization, the snake enthroned on its seat of power. They had not yet seen the snake within, quietly waiting to poison paradise.

At last the captain came. He parked his battered red Datsun pickup on the wharf—the only car allowed to park on the wharf. Its muffler poked straight up out of the hood through a hole he had cut. He stalked scowling down the ramp, looking neither left nor right, climbed up into the wheel house and revved the engine. Everyone followed him aboard. In the salon it still smelled faintly of yesterday's vomit.

"Salon" sounds elegant, like something from a transatlantic ocean liner, but the only resemblance would have been to the Titanic—and it wouldn't have been about the décor. The salon was a small compartment whose roof was held up by several rusting iron poles. The floor was of chipped linoleum tile, the ceiling of sagging acoustic tiles—the kind full of little holes. Six unmatched couches, three on either side of the aisle, were covered with blankets to mask their shabbiness. It was part of the deckhand's job to straighten the blankets each day. Often, in high seas, the blanket-covered couches slid back and forth, and people just stretched out on them in a comatose trance. Occasionally someone would retch into a barf bag or onto the floor. Mopping up after a rough crossing was also the deckhand's job.

Ryan walked past the couches and climbed the three steps at the stern of the boat. He pushed open the double wooden doors and stepped out onto the little open deck that the Captain called "the latterine." He preferred to ride out back rather than in the stuffy salon. In rough seas he enjoyed balancing on the deck without touching the railing. His cowboy hat was crammed down tight over his head to keep it from blowing off. His dark face was framed by his beard and by the nimbus of long curly hair that protruded out from under the hat. His brown eyes gazed at the horizon. It was like Tai Chi, this using your sea legs to flow back and forth with the rise and fall of the waves.

The ferry backed in a great circle out into the bay, turning to face Vancouver Island. Then the Captain shoved it into forward and started the hour long voyage. Usually some other passengers came out back to talk or share a joint. Today Ryan was the only one on the back deck. He watched the flat-calm sea with its odd bits of flotsam pass by. The sun broke through for a moment and lighted up the shores and mountains of Vancouver Island; then it was grey again.

On the other shore, after the deckhand had tied the ferry to the float, Ryan got off with the other passengers. He walked up to the parking lot to find his antique grey Epic Envoy, hoping it had not had its gas siphoned or been looted for parts. The parking lot was an open field covered with gravel and frozen puddles. He tiptoed over the ice, trying not to break through on his way to the car. For a long time after Sheila left with their shiny blue Datsun pickup, Ryan had hitched with a pack on his back or borrowed one of his friend's disreputable cars. He had bought the Envoy for three hundred dollars from a woman raising cash to go to Guatemala. He was simply happy to have a car again.

The drive down to Victoria was a panorama of coast and trees. There were a few dreary suburbs, but there was also Nanoose, with its high bluffs, submarines, and long grey bay. There was the Malahat, a shimmering two lane mountain highway winding above islands and waterways. Near the top of the Malahat, Ryan pulled over and stopped for a toke. Below him was Finlayson

Arm and, beyond it, the Saanich peninsula with its checkerboard of farms. Ryan looked over the winter landscape, trees, fields, clouds, and mountains, and thought that winter was when God slept; that he, Ryan, was the dreamer, a living remnant of consciousness, driving his car through God's frozen sleep.

A few snowflakes began to fall and Ryan pulled back out on the highway, wanting to get to Hirsh's before it began to stick. By the time he got to the three way fork on Old West Saanich—where the white church is—the snow was falling thickly. His tires left twin black marks in the whitening road. Ryan thought that the church looked like a scene in one of those glass balls that you shake to watch the snowflakes fall. A crystal ball. He scried into it, and wondered, in this last mile, what his trip would bring.

He came to the overgrown hedge, a tangled mass of holly, snow berry, blackberry, hardhack, Oregon grape, hawthorn, and young alders, that gave Hirsh the privacy that he needed to live his strange life. The day was fading into twilight.

Ryan was excited to see a light shining through the snow-traced hedge; excited that someone was home. Hirsh was usually at the farm, but Ryan did have some fear of arriving to a lonely, cold house. Ryan had tried calling from the payphone at the store, but had gotten the message that "the number you are calling is no longer in service." It did not surprise him, as Hirsh often did not have the money to pay his bills. Ryan was craving light, wine, company, conversation, the stories and jokes at which Hirsh was so good. He drove into the virgin snow of the farmyard and saw that there were no tire tracks, just the snow and the settling of night. Hirsh's ancient truck was gone, but an equally antique, much travelled looking Hillman Minx with Oregon plates was parked in its place. Ryan parked and got out of his car.

Almost immediately Hirsh's two strange dogs, Pumpkin Feathers and Snartch, came bounding down from the porch to check him out. For anyone else this would have been alarming: Pumpkin Feathers was large, white, short-haired and had a furtive look about her. She looked like a dog drawn by a Flemish surrealist. All she needed was wings to be some nightmarish detail from a lost Bosch painting. She had already run down the paper boy and pulled him off his bike; Ryan couldn't understand why she hadn't been put down yet. Snartch, a German Shepherd, was by contrast, hangdog and pleading. He limped painfully along on his broken hind quarters.

Ryan thought of a passage in the Castaneda books, where Don Juan, the shaman, and his apprentice Carlito are sitting on a cliff top in the dead of night. They are listening to the distant howling of a dog. Don Juan whispers to Carlito: "At night while the man sleeps, his soul goes forth in the body of the dog and howls for release. Ryan wondered if perhaps these two dogs, the black one and the white one, embodied the parts of Hirsh that were too uncool to express in mellow hippy culture, his aggression and his woundedness. The Castaneda books were taken as gospel back then. Why is one gospel always replaced by another?

At any rate, Snartch and Pumpkin Feathers were like mythical beasts that guarded Hirsh's archetypal, drug induced world against incursions from reality. They recognised Ryan almost immediately and gave up their barking. Instead they danced and pranced around him, jumping up on him with wet paws, yelping and making little whining sounds. Even Snartch managed a prance or two. The snow was churned up into a confusion of paw prints and boot marks. Ryan was shouting, "DOWN, DOWN," at the top of his lungs. When the dogs were more or less under control, he walked through the drifting snow towards the light from the kitchen window, the dogs bouncing and jouncing around him.

He walked up the back stairs and knocked on the kitchen door. Much to his surprise his knock was answered by a lithe and beautiful woman. She had arisen from her warm place by the oil stove where she had been watching his arrival and the ensuing scene with the dogs. Her face was flushed with laughter.

"Hi, I am Ryan, is Hirsh here?"

"Hi, I'm Selene, no. Pumpkin Feathers, DOWN, OUT." She gestured fiercely toward the door with her arm.

The dogs slunk back but then kept trying to squeeze into the warm house around and through Ryan's legs. With a mixture of exasperation and laughter that Ryan liked, she shoved them back out on to the porch.

"Come on in," she said, "come in quickly." She said it warmly but also a bit crossly. Ryan realised that she wanted to close the door against the dogs and weather.

He came into the house and saw that she was cold, had bundled up in sweaters and barricaded herself in the warm kitchen. She had been sitting at Hirsh's Salvation Army table with her chair pulled up close to the oil stove. Ryan could see the hole that she had wiped in the steamy window to watch his arrival. There was a chipped tea pot at her place, an equally chipped cup half full of tea and an open frayed paperback upside down on the table.

"Would you like some tea?"

"Yea, far-out, that sounds great."

She pulled another chair around the table, closer to the oil stove, closer to her. She took the great aluminum kettle from the top of the oil stove and poured fresh hot water into the pot. She added another spoon of tea from a Chinese tin on the counter.

Ryan sat in his chair, too cold to take his coat off, but he unbuttoned it as a gesture of staying awhile. He had also taken off the large light-grey Stetson that he wore with the crown puffed out, Tom Mix style. He had found it in a second hand store in Centralia, Oregon and had painted a fierce face on the crown with black waterproof ink. It was a psychedelic face, fractured into Picasso-like planes, that grinned out above his own mild Byzantine eyes.

When his friend McElwaith saw the painting he said, "Shit, man, why did you ruin a perfectly good hat?" The hat sat on the kitchen table where it stared out at both of them. It was dusted with snowflakes that were melting into small dark freckles. The fly-away ends of Ryan's long, almost frizzy hair that had been sticking out beyond the brim of the hat were still dusted with melting snowflakes.

"Hirsh went to Vancouver to visit his brother. He'll be back sometime tomorrow." Hirsh's brother was the one who had done well in the family, a psychologist who looked a lot like Hirsh. Ryan felt slightly uneasy:

Who was this Selene? Was he welcome? Was he an intrusion? She was very beautiful and Ryan always felt uneasy around beautiful women. Anyway, tea was served and Ryan decided to take it minute by minute instead of trying to figure everything out right away. This was the new art that he had been learning, "going with the flow," living in the here and now and letting decisions come from the texture of the moment, rather than trying to have life all figured out in advance.It was about letting life unfold, rather than directing it; about letting go of the reins to see where the horse would take you; about getting lost, but trusting that in so doing you would find things of greater interest than those to which the limited intellect could lead.

Ryan was moving from seeing life as something that humans created and moulded to their satisfaction, to seeing it as a great creative being of which they were just a part. It was based on the notion that the evolutionary process that had created them was still unfolding, and, if he learned how to sense and surrender to it, would guide him to completion. This, though perhaps Ryan couldn't have named it yet, was the paradigm shift that they all were living. They were learning how to go with the flow, ride with the tide, ooze with the gooze and suck with the muck.

Half way through tea—with just a little chuckle—Selene asked Ryan if he wanted to smoke a little dope. "I was just going to smoke some myself," was the way she put it, and "would you like to join me?" She opened a small ornate box that was sitting innocently on the worn kitchen table. The box was oval and had a cloisonné Persian bird on its lapis-coloured lid. She pulled the ubiquitous package of Zig-Zag blues out of it and a few Eddy Red Bird Strike-Anywhere matches. She reached into it with her long fingers and began placing crumbs of marijuana in the creased valley of the paper that she was holding with her other hand. When its little trench was full, she rolled the paper into a narrow cylinder, raised it to her mouth, and delicately licked the glue strip with the tip of her tongue. Her long light brown hair, parted in the middle, fell forward as she did this. After pressing down the glue strip, she twisted the ends shut so the precious substance wouldn't fall out. She put the whole joint in her mouth to wet it lightly so that the paper wouldn't burn faster than the grass inside it. Then, tossing her hair back, she placed the joint in her mouth, struck one of the matches against the bottom of the table and lit it. She took a deep toke and passed it to Ryan. They held the smoke in their lungs and made the peculiar little choking and sucking sounds that were part of dope smoking. Ryan held the smoking joint above his cupped palm so that the ashes wouldn't fall on the table. Finally, like orcas surfacing, they blew out what was left of the clouds of smoke they had inhaled. They were coughing and laughing at the same time. Ryan passed the joint back to her.

It went back and forth this way until there was nothing left but the small resin stained roach. Selene took her roach clip—a small tweezers with a blue bead fastened to it—out of her cloisonné box and gripped the roach with it. She slipped the bead up over the prongs so that the roach was locked in place. Again, they passed it back and forth, holding it by the clip. This time they held it slightly out from their mouths and sucked forcefully, creating a venturi effect that made the roach glow and spark. The roach was supposed to be the strongest part of the joint, reputed to contain all the resins that had previously passed through it. Selene tipped her head slightly back as she drew on the roach. She tucked her hair behind her ears and let it flow down her back. They continued to go through the ritual of holding the smoke in for as long as they could, letting every molecule enter their brains. When the roach was gone they sat in stoned silence. Finally, they both said, "Wow!" at the same time.

Now, as they sat beside the oil stove, their tongues and minds loosened, who they really were, began to

16

flow back and forth. Ryan started to feel comfortable rather than like an intruding stranger. Was not this meant to be happening in the great unfolding tapestry? Had it not been in the cards this morning, in the snow that fell outside, in the ornate box and the matches on the table, in Hirsh's convenient absence? Ryan thought to himself, "if you can apply willing suspension of disbelief to theatre, why not to life itself?"

So Ryan sat with this beautiful woman in the one warm room of a freezing farmhouse. He felt an ease come over him, a desire to talk and share his stories, his jokes, his little plays on words with Selene, this woman who was full of both laughter and crusty scepticism. They mocked and made fun of the ritual they had just been through; said "far-out" with just the right degree of irony; laughed at the linguistic level to which they had fallen.

II
In The Kitchen

The cold closed in around them. They sat in the unadorned kitchen, surrounded by its glacial white walls, its bare light bulb, its red plastic wall clock grinding away the hours. She opened the oven door to let more heat into the room; she took the burner lifter and lifted the round cast-iron plate to eye the flame; she twisted the dial on the side of the stove and banged on the control box to see if she could get more heat. She walked to the door and let the dogs in, taking them by their collars and making them lie down under the table.

Ryan watched her and noted a litheness that was visible even under her layers of warm clothing: a combination of sensual languor and athletic decisiveness that underlay all her gestures. She pulled her chair to the other side of the oven door and sat down putting her feet up on the open door. "Try it," she said with a shiver, "it's the only way to stay warm."

Ryan moved his chair around to the other side of the oven door. He took off his big logger boots and placed his stockinged feet on the warm metal, just short of hers. She leaned out and took her tea from the table and continued to sip it. He did the same. They sat quietly facing each other, their feet up on the oven door. The snow continued to fall and the darkness deepened outside the window. The dogs had fallen asleep and were twitching under the table.

"My sisters and I used to have foot fights," he offered. "We used to sit on the floor opposite each other, like this, and push with our legs to see who could push the other back." He very tentatively put the sole of one stockinged foot against one of hers and gave a gentle token push to illustrate what he was saying. She pushed back, just for an instant and they both laughed and then gave the game up. He pulled his foot back to his side of the oven door, but contact had been made and with the mention of his sisters, the richness of their histories began to unfold.

They shared much in common. They both were Americans. "Yeah, I grew up in eastern Oregon," she said, "surrounded by open spaces. Ever been to eastern Oregon? It's not forests, like the coast. Its crinkled hills covered with sagebrush. As a girl I always felt the presence of the Indians. I was fascinated when I saw them in town. I read books about them and searched the hills for artifacts. I read books about herbs and learned how to find them. It was like I grew up surrounded by the spirit and bones of the Klamath people. My great grandparents came out on the Oregon Trail and cut a homestead out of the forest. They had stories to tell about the Indians. My dad moved east, into the desert. I don't think he ever liked the forest. Too much darkness for him. He didn't have any brothers or sisters."

Ryan studied her intelligent blue eyes as she told him this; he looked at the curve of her nose, the arch of her eyebrows, the quizzical turn to her mouth, her slightly elfin ears. She got up to add more tea to the pot and poured again from the great kettle that bubbled away on the stove. She refilled it and put it back on the stove, leaving the tap dribbling to keep it from freezing. "He worked for the Department of Agriculture. Irrigating the desert, making things grow, that sort of thing. My mom was a librarian. Part time. Most of the time she stayed home and worked on this historical novel that turned into an interminable history of everything on the American frontier. I remember playing outside as a girl, and seeing her through the window typing away. When I came up here I told her 'You better finish it one of these days. Don't expect me to publish it for you after you're gone.'"

Fair warning, Ryan thought. But he said, "far out, my grandfather, Guiseppi, came out from Italy. When I was seventeen I used to pick up a bottle of muscatel on the way to my girlfriend's house in SF and stop by his flat to have a drink with him. We sat at the kitchen table and drank out of these little faceted Italian wineglasses that looked like jam jars."

He leaned out and refilled his tea cup from the pot on the table. He slurped his tea through open lips, sucking it in so as not to burn himself. "He was hard to understand. After all his years in The States he still spoke almost no English. As the eldest son, he had come out to California with his father to work in the mines and bring money back to Italy. After several trips he saved up and bought land, sight unseen, in Arizona. I think he was thinking about the kind of small farm he came from. He went by train to claim the land that he had finally been able to buy. The realtor took him and some other immigrants out to their land. As he stood there in the blinding glare of this barren place, nothing at all like the green terraced hills of Liguria where he was born, he noticed Indians, 'looking out from behind cactuses,' he said. The realtor told him and the other immigrants 'Just shoot them if they get in your way.' It was another one of those great immigrant land deals. He climbed back on the train, his small fortune gone. 'The land wasn't worth killing for,' was what he said to me. He worked as a janitor for the rest of his life. He sent for his family and

21

managed to buy a flat in SF. In his old age he was finally able to buy a few acres in Sonoma county. Our parents put a trailer on his land and we used to hang out there as kids. He grew vegetables and brought them back to the city to sell at the corner store below his house in North Beach."

Thus they whiled away the evening. The snow was now too deep to drive out and buy food, so they cooked what they could find in Hirsh's refrigerator. This was a dangerous proposition that involved much opening of jars and sniffing at them. They found some rice to cook, some eggs for an omelettes and vegetables for the filling. The wiltedness of the vegetables was not too apparent once they had been diced and sautéed. They even found half a jug of wine that Hirsh had left behind.

As the house creaked and contracted around them, the cold pushed them closer together. The only warm place was the circle around the oil stove. Hirsh had apparently not had enough money to fill the tank of the enormous furnace that lurked like a multi-armed monster in the basement.

As they made and ate dinner, they shared stories of their childhood, of their parents, of their grandparents. Selene was also an astrologer. She carried a bale of ephemerides (she called them "ephemerises") around with her, large floppy books with pale blue paper covers.

22

They showed the positions of all the planets at any given moment of birth. After dinner they cleared away the dishes and scrubbed the table. She cast a rough horoscope for Ryan, drawing it on the back of one of Hirsh's three month old unpaid Hydro bills. She used a chipped blue bowl as a template for drawing the circle. Ryan did not know the moment of his birth, but, from the day, she cast a tentative chart. It looked like a spider web with planets hanging in it like captured bugs.

"Without your exact time of birth I can't tell you the location of your moon." she told him, "It governs your emotions and unconscious. It changes its place in the zodiac every two hours. We also don't know your rising sign." She drew a horizon line through the center of the chart and pointed at it with her pencil. "The constellation of the Zodiac that is on the horizon at the moment of your birth," she explained. "It governs your physical appearance and the face you show the world, your persona."

To Ryan, she was an astrologer-magician, looking into his soul under the bare bulb of the winter kitchen. The dark world outside—farmland and forest—spread frozen around them. The real moon and stars were obscured by layers of flurrying cloud. It felt like they were people who had been transported from another time, who had learned, in all too short a time, to wear ragged clothes and drive ancient cars.

There was much more to astrology than Ryan had supposed. Selene told him how each of the twelve signs fit into one of the four primal elements, Earth, Air, Fire or Water. "Within each element there are three signs that represent the different phases of each element: Cardinal, Fixed and Mutable. For example, in your element, Fire, there is cardinal Aries, the first wild expression of fire; fixed Leo, your sign, the mature stable version of it; and mutable Sagittarius. She looked at him frequently to see if he was following. He saw the deep blue of her eyes. "Mutable means fire spreading out into all the other elements, influencing and being influenced by them. It's like the delta of a great river where it fans out to join the sea."

She showed him, under the bare bulb, his soul's journey through the progression of the signs; the different lessons to be learned from the lifetimes spent in each sign. She pulled out a deck of cards from a blue velvet bag on the table. It was the second time he had seen the Tarot that day. She lay out the Major Arcana against the signs of the Zodiac. "It begins with The Fool who is walking along, his head in the clouds. What do you see about him?"

"He's about to step off the edge of a cliff. There is a little white dog yapping at his feet, trying to warn him."

"Yes," she said, "Even the Fool is sustained by invisible forces of spirit that are looking after him, though he doesn't know it yet." She sat back in her chair and seemed to chuckle a bit about the plight of the poor Fool.

Ryan, his head lost in a cloud of marijuana, felt that he had already walked off the cliff; that he had fallen into a medieval view of the world. His university training had taught him to dismiss all this as pseudo-science, this idea of a journeying soul that was connected to the planets and stars, holographically connected to everything in the universe and influenced by the Zodiac.

"Zodiac is from the Greek word zoidion," said Selene, "it originally meant little clay animals." Selene had learned all this in Eugene, Oregon, where she used to live with her boyfriend. She had learned it from a chiropractor who taught astrology and Tarot in the evening after he had finished cracking backs for the day.

When the wine ran out they made more steaming pots of green tea. They peered out from time to time through the hole they were keeping open in the window's frozen condensation. Drifts of snow clustered on the window sills. Their cars were barely visible in the porch light. They had become white haystacks in the swirling maelstrom of the night.

III
Let's Go to Bed

Selene yawned and looked at the red plastic clock grinding away on the wall. Its hands were moving toward two a.m. The table was covered with cups, Tarot cards, ephemerides, and planetary notations that looked like Einstein theorems. "Let's go to bed," she said. She got up decisively, opened the door and beckoned Ryan through it into the rest of the dark and frozen house. She led the way, flicking on the light as they passed through the Salvation Army furniture of the frozen living room. Hirsh's collection of rock posters from the San Franciso Renaissance lined the walls. The Grateful Dead's brightly coloured psychedelic skulls looked down at Selene and Ryan from their auras of light; Posada's dancing skeletons offered them glasses of wine and roses. They walked past the open door to Hirsh's bedroom with its unmade bed and piles of clothes on the floor, past the bathroom where the taps were dripping to keep the pipes from freezing. Everything was frozen and cold. The house felt like a castle under a spell.

27

Winding through the rooms, they arrived at the frozen sun porch that was Selene's bedroom. It was the room where Ryan usually stayed when he visited Hirsh. He had slept alone in its single bed many times while the house around him had shaken to the sounds of Hirsh and his latest woman in the other room. The sun porch stuck out from the side of the house and had big mullioned windows on three sides. Below the windows was clapboard wainscoting. It was just big enough for a single bed and a chair to pile clothes on.

The small chaste bed was mounded with Selene's down sleeping bag. She had covered it with other blankets scrounged from around the house. Her collection of arrowheads and small beaded pouches lined the window sills. Small bundles of dried herbs hung from the curtain rods. Ryan had learned in their long hours of wine and tea drinking that she had a degree in ethnobotany. "Yeah, and what am I going to do with that?" is what she had said, her hands held out to the side in a gesture of mock helplessness.

On the wall was a small daguerreotype of a woman in long skirts climbing onto a buggy. One foot and one hand were already up on the buggy; her other hand was holding the buggy whip. "My Grandmother," Selene said when she saw Ryan looking at it.

Everything in the room was fastidious and neatly arranged. It was like a nucleus of sanity in the cytoplasmic chaos of Hirsh's house. "You can sleep here with me tonight if you would like, maybe we will even be able to keep each other warm." Her words vibrated through Ryan electrically. He did not know whether she was simply suggesting that they huddle together for warmth or that they would make love. He simply accepted her offer. Go with the flow. She went back to turn out the living room light. When she returned, she clicked out the light to her room. Even in the darkness, the pale light of the snow shone through the ice crusted windows.

"There must be a moon up there behind the clouds," Ryan whispered in a shivery voice.

"There is." she said, "It's full and in Scorpio."

It was too cold and frozen to even think about taking off clothes. They simply climbed into bed. After a moment of embarrassment they climbed into each other's arms, chattering and shivering. Ryan had a vision of them being found frozen in their embrace, a cold version of the figures at Pompeii.

Little by little they warmed up. The down lofted and trapped their heat. They pulled the covers over their heads and warmed the bed with their breath. As Ryan became warm, a strong current of desire began to flow through him. Selene seemed to press closer and his body awakened. Their shivering had stopped. Ryan just lay there for awhile enjoying the thrill of the energy that was flowing through him; the thrill of strangers meeting; the thrill of their youth, freedom, and beauty. He began to stroke her back through the layers of sweaters and turtlenecks. "OK?" he asked. "Ummmm," she replied.

Their bodies pressed closer. Occasionally her hand reached up to his neck to find his bare skin. She let her fingers graze here, sending shivers down his body. Pressed together like flowers in a book, they clung to each other in their winter clothes. The vast muffling silence of the snow was punctuated by little sighs and umms. They lay in their current of ecstasy until light sleep carried them away. They floated in and out of sleep, awakening to each other, to caresses and the sweetness of each other's breath.

It was as though the night, the storm, the snow, Hirsh's convenient absence, had all conspired to bring them together; as though the world laughed, the frozen winter laughed; even the Scorpio moon, high above the billowing storm, smiled beneficently down as they lay in each other's arms. In one of his brief slides into sleep, Ryan dreamed that the figures of the Tarot had come to life and were wandering around the house. They were somewhat transparent, like brightly coloured ghosts. In the attic, the Sun, liberated from its box of cards, hung under the rafters radiantly warming the frozen rooms below. In the living room the Lovers sat entwined on the couch, while in the kitchen the Priestess talked to the beautiful Angel of Temperance. They seemed oblivious to the lobster from the Moon card, a pair of ragged claws, scuttling around the kitchen looking for crumbs. Out in the frozen farmyard, the Hermit kept his lonely vigil, holding his lantern aloft over empty fields of snow, while Death's white horse stamped restlessly in the barn. Far away on the crest of the hill that overlooked the farm, a King and Queen were pouring tea in a small room high atop a tall stone tower.

IV
Sliding Around

In the morning they bundled up and walked down the stairs into the snowy world. They dug their cars out enough to climb in and see if they would start. Ryan's Epic groaned slowly in the frozen morning. Selene's Minx did just a little better. They dug it out the rest of the way and sprayed some ether into the carburetor from a can they found in the barn. The Minx roared into life, laying a thick white fog of condensed exhaust across the snowy barnyard. Laughingly, they dug a track to the road. With a couple of bags of hardened concrete in its trunk for traction, the Minx pushed its way out onto the road. It was a growly little car, full of spark and persistence, seemingly determined to make up for its small size with sheer strength of will. Around them, the occasional orange snowplough clanked along the deserted thoroughfares; the world was white, pristine and mounded; full of drifts and snow covered roofs.

They drove across the peninsula to visit Thom and Daphne, the friends that Selene had followed to Victoria.

Thom and Daphne lived in a small house, perhaps once a gardener's cottage, on the grounds of a mansion on a slope high above Todd Inlet. Friends of theirs rented the main house and had sublet the cottage to them. They had named the property Peralandra, after CS Lewis' planet of love.

Stone paths wound through rockeries and extensive gardens. In spring the garden was abloom with azalea, daffodils and tulips; in summer full of perennials; now, in winter's last gasp, it was bare, with only a few waxy green leaves showing above the snow.

That evening, after dinner, they all drove out to the local pub to spend hours in crazy conversation. At some point Ryan got up from the round table full of empties and walked cautiously to the washroom, trying not to stagger. Selene watched him. When he returned she smiled. Leaning into him and gently taking his arm, she whispered: "You walk with your chin sticking out, like you're inviting the world to take a punch at you."

That night, back at Hirsh's, they slept together without so many clothes. She wore a cotton gown that was really a long undershirt. Its thin knit cloth clung to her body. Immobilised by long, slow kisses, they stayed pressed to each other in aching arousal. Their bodies seemed to flow together through the pores of their skin. Illuminated by the intensity of their longing, they grazed each other's bodies with only the lightest touch of their fingers. It was as though they themselves were transparent and too solid a touch could break the illusion and make them disappear back into the thin air.

At the height of arousal they stopped and lay perfectly still. It felt like the normal pathways of their bodies could no longer contain the voltage that they had accumulated and it spread out through all their cells. They twitched a little and drifted off into a trance full of surprising shared dreams and images. They fell into deep sleep and awakened in each other's arms, on fire, and shared their dreams. Then they started again until another trance took them deeper. They spent hours under the down bag as the frozen days and nights inched on around them. They became achingly close, achingly responsive to each other's touch or glance. Nature's unfinished business coursed through them.

Hirsh still had not returned. "I'll bet he's enjoying his brother's nice warm house," said Selene, "and has no intention of coming back until this is over." When all this became too much, they once again pulled on their many layers of clothes, put the dogs in the back seat, and sprayed more ether into the Minx's carburettor.

"It is a trick I learned here in the frozen north," said Ryan.

They both knew that it was a joke to call Victoria the frozen north.

"But in the Provincial guidebook," she lectured, "it says that 'the Gulf of Georgia represents the furthest northward manifestation of a true Mediterranean climate.'" She made the quotes sound like the soundtrack from a travelogue.

Ryan had never seen the Mediterranean, but he felt that his Italian genes—and his shivering body—entitled him to say: "That sounds like a load of academic hogwash to me."

They spent some days sliding around the Saanich Peninsula, driving to and from Thom and Daphne's. The white, rolling landscape was divided into agricultural squares by hedgerows of naked blackberry, snowberry, and hawthorn. At Peralandra, the long driveway curved down from West Saanich Road through cedars to the house below. Since there was no way the Hillman would get back up the icy driveway, Selene and Ryan parked at the top and walked down through a Christmas card landscape of snow encrusted trees. Large snowflakes floated down around them. They clung to each other so as not to fall on the ice and yelled at the dogs to get them to behave.

They spent long candle lit evenings with Thom and Daphne, drinking wine, smoking dope, cooking sumptuous dinners together and indulging in wild conversation. Sometimes, out of pity, they brought in Hirsh's unruly dogs. Daphne let them stay in a little laundry room behind the kitchen, as long as they lay down and behaved.

Thom was large, phlegmatic, matter of fact, full of knowledge, facts and information. He had short, curly reddish hair, blue eyes, and a squarish head. "The very picture of a Leo rising," Selene told Ryan when they were alone. Daphne was mercurial, had long dark hair, laughed easily, and was an anthropologist. Selene said that she was a Cancer, "fond of home and comfort."

Their friend Tim, also living with them, was a Canadian.

"What's your sign?"

"I'm a Canadian."

He was a veteran of both logging camps and Zen monasteries and equally at home in both, not seeming to distinguish between them. On the long nights he told them stories about the Zen masters he had survived: "Yea, once I sat stoned on acid at an all day sesshin. The acid was peaking and I was freaking. The room absolutely silent, full of people sitting like statues on their cushions. Like, I felt I was about to explode, about to start screaming and run out of the room. I desperately centered myself, focused my concentration on my hara. I watched my breath go in and out of my belly. After awhile I opened my eyes. The old Japanese Roshi had his eyes open and was staring right at me. Our eyes locked and he whispered to me, in his bad English, 'No use cling to navel. In end she ripped away too.' Then he closed his eyes again. It was the only time he spoke during the meditation.

"At the beginning of the retreat he collected our money and then left us milling around in the unshaded courtyard. In a couple of hours everyone was sweating, grumbling and unhappy. He came out on the balcony waving a fistful of our money. Some of the bills slipped out of his fingers and fluttered to the ground like paper airplanes. He brandished his handful of cash and cheques and shouted at us. 'You may think I crazy old man, ha, ha, ha, but I no care 'cause I got your money, ha, ha, ha, I got your money!' Then he disappeared, laughing crazily, into the coolness of the monastery. And that was just for starters."

"By the end, when everyone was all sparkly and transcendent, all smiley and talking in hushed tones, he came flapping in with six packs tucked under the arms of his robe and rings of polish sausage festooned around his neck. He insisted we all join him for beer and sausage.

"Yeah man, it was all good training for the logging camps. I get up in the dark, before anyone is awake, and sit cross legged in my bunk. I eat my steak and sausage with the rest of 'em, fall trees all day, and wash my supper down with whisky at night."

Selene, in response, brightly sang a variation on a little children's song: "I'm a lumberjack and I'm ok, I drink all night and work all day."

Ryan said, "Yeah, man, with a Zen twinkle in your eye, right?"

"Yeah, with a Zen twinkle."

When they first came to Canada, Selene's friends had worked for a Free School on one of the Gulf Islands. It was an experiment in radical education. The school was later disbanded after a plot had been discovered to blow up the power lines that crossed the island. They had hoped to stop the power that flowed from the drowned valleys of the interior to the television sets of Vancouver Island. It was a political science project whose premise was: "Unplug them and they will discover who they are."

Selene, Thom, Daphne, Tim and Ryan spent the blue twilight afternoons smoking dope, casting horoscopes, and doing Tarot readings. In the cottage above Todd Inlet, blue light leaked out of the snow banks and painted the living room in winter colours. Everything looked like Picasso's blue phase. They entered deeply into each other's lives, discussing how this symbol or that archetype fit or didn't fit. They saw The Fool, The Magician, and The Priestess in each other. They talked about The Chariot, how each of them must balance the black and white beast within to keep their lives running straight.

As the late snow continued to fall, they looked at the royal figures of the King and Queen falling from their burning tower. They talked about the times when the carefully created structures of their lives—plans, relationships, livelihoods—had been struck by lightning and they had been cast from the secure towers that they had tried to create, cast down to beg and pray and ask the sky for help. They were only in their early twenties but so much had already happened.

They talked about The Five of Pentacles, the poverty card, which shows a crippled beggar, wrapped in rags, hobbling on his crutches in the snow. They talked about the fat man with the half gnawed drumstick holding on to coins with both his hands and feet. They talked about The Moon card with its howling dog and its crayfish scuttling out of the water. They talked about poverty, greed, and evolution; about their efforts to become less animal and more human, or was it more godlike?

They even looked at each other's hands, the lines on them, the shape of them, the length and taper of their fingers. As the last dark days of winter inched forward and the frozen year crept toward the rebirth of Spring, they played at inferring from each other's hands what kind of person each of them was and what each was becoming.

Selene was their guide. Not an arrogant guide full of great knowingness, The Hierophant, but a guide with a cardboard box full of books who was willing to flip through and find the answers to their questions. It was the academic, well researched approach to the occult. The time passed richly as each short day passed into long electrically lit evenings full of conversation. Used to the sleepiness of kerosene lamps, the evenings were a pleasure for Ryan. He endlessly watched Selene as she sat curled up in one of the old easy chairs, eating vegetarian pizza or making notes as she pored through her books. Her baggy clothes didn't quite conceal the lines of her body.

They all spent large parts of each snowy day sprawled on the old furniture, turning pages, occasionally sharing some occult gem with each other: five brains working together as one great brain, trying to puzzle out this ancient vision of the universe, the lost map upon which they had stumbled. It was a magic lens through which their lives took on meanings beyond the mundane ones of working, eating, making money, sleeping, having sex, raising children, growing old, dying. They were like a team of explorers gathering information about the journey they were on.

For Ryan, it was as though a door had opened and a whole new world had appeared: the ancient world upon which the modern world, a flashy veneer of machines, fast food and facile scientific explanations, had merely been superimposed. It was the ultimate in delicious disorientation. The whole world spun on the tip of his finger. He felt like The Magician, juggling infinity.

He even liked the struggle that went on inside him between belief and disbelief: he was not really sure whether he believed that astrology was a determinant of each person's character and place on their spiritual journey. Perhaps it was just a map of character or a metaphor for spiritual growth disguised as fortune telling. Selene just laughed and said that it was normal for him to think this way because he had Mercury in Virgo. She told him that Mercury ruled the mind and Virgo was given to rational thought, detail, logic and proving things. After she told it to him, Ryan delighted in explaining that he didn't believe in Astrology because he had Mercury in Virgo.

Thom and Ryan were the rational sceptics of the bunch, constantly chiding the rest of them that the whole system was out of whack. Ryan had learned to recognise Leo in a college physical science class, and had seen it blazing in the August sky, long after sunset, when it should have, if the ephemerides were right, already set with the sun. He had seen for himself that the Zodiac of astrology didn't correspond to the actual position of the sun in the heavens.

Selene sighed. She said that astrologers understood this, that they knew it was because of the precession of the equinoxes, but that it had been difficult to update the system because all the Leos—she looked accusingly at Ryan—considered themselves to be the very best of signs, and couldn't face the fact that they were really Cancer's. They viewed it as a downgrading of their unique status, she said, and were extremely resistant to revising the system. She shrugged. "Ultimately, it really doesn't matter that signs don't correspond with physical reality: they are thought forms and supersede it".

"Wait a minute! Are you saying that ultimately it's the fault of reality, not of astrology; that the plan of the heavens spins around us in its divine perfection, casting down platonic ideals that can only be crudely approximated on the physical plane? Are you saying 'so what' to the fact that the sun isn't actually in the sign it's supposed to be in? What does it matter?"

"Yeah, I guess I am. Something like that."

But for Ryan this was a matter for serious consideration. "Twelve pulses, twelve signs, twelve months, twelve apostles, twelve Zhang-Fu. What is it with the number twelve?"

"Duodecimal," said Thom, "a great round number system built on twelve. It fits as cleanly into the solar system as a Frank Lloyd Wright house fits into a hill side. It's built to explain the roundness of creation rather than the rectilinear cubes of modern civilisation. The way you think determines what you believe."

"What number can you never say in public?"

"I dunno, what?"

"288—aren't you going to ask me why?"

"OK, why?"

"Because it's two gross."

Ryan tried to distinguish the glimpse of a greater reality that gleamed out through the chinks in metaphysical knowledge, from puerile superstition. Which was which? Ah, the curse of Mercury in Virgo. Was marijuana slowly prising open his mind-forged manacles, he wondered, or was it just replacing them with another more ornate set? He began to see the world through the lens of twelve rather than that of ten. He simply said "far out" a lot of the time, often without irony.

Sometimes Selene and Ryan spent the night rather than drive home through the slippery landscape. They pushed the table back and put a small mattress down on the floor of a little dining room off the kitchen. They heaped it high with coverlets, blankets, whatever was around. They closed the glass paned doors and the room became theirs. They had graduated to love making now, but in a long, slow way, lying still in each other's arms and passing into dreams. When they awakened, they moved a little to fan the flames. As they approached climax they stopped and drifted into dreams again, lying in each other's arms while their spirits wandered. Lovemaking was an intense pleasure and also a gateway to somewhere else.

Selene had opened a huge door for Ryan, introduced him to a metaphysical world that all his life he had shunned—a world that had been labelled "pseudo-science" in university—that had been pointed at and ridiculed. Ryan discovered that though lacking in verifiable reality, it contained the satisfying mythic truth for which he had long been searching. The world ceased to be flat. Or maybe it ceased to be round. All around him were connections to the great invisible world that he had momentarily seen, on his first Acid trip, as a great wheel turning through everything, even through his own flesh.

Ryan also realised that Selene didn't really give a fig whether he believed or not. Her affection for him was built on something entirely different. This was new to him, a love that was not based on alliance, on loyalty, on bolstering each other up; a love that was full of dangerous freedom and let-be.

And then the rains came, pelting Northwest Coast rains full of large rain drops that fell on everything like fat spiders. The snow was gone as quickly as it had come. Selene, Thom, Daphne, Tim and Ryan, stood under the overhang of the cottage where they had spent their days and nights together. They watched the colour green re-emerge into the world as if by a trick of Raven. Suddenly, instead of snow drifts, they were surrounded by rosettes of sword fern that had been flattened by the snow and by springy, glistening salal. Everywhere, the incipient buds of spring were swelling and waiting to burst. Daffodil and Tulip tips pushed up out of the earth. Even Hirsh's dogs stood with them, sniffing the world as it emerged from the snow and watching the rain fall. What would a long house be without the dogs?

Hirsh came looking for them. He had returned from luxury living in Vancouver to find his dogs gone, his house unheated, his phone disconnected, his new roommate, the flighty woman from Oregon, gone. He saw Ryan's lifeless Epic in the driveway and set out to find them. He was surprised and mildly annoyed that no-one had bought oil for the great furnace under the house.

Everyone went their separate ways. It was as though some new cog in the celestial wheel had clicked into place. The show was over: they must all move now, strike their tents. Selene and Ryan caravanned back to the farm with Hirsh. His ancient International truck went first with the dogs in the back. Selene's Minx followed close on its tailgate. Inside, Selene and Ryan held hands and marveled at the drippy green world around them.

Back at the farm Hirsh helped Ryan jumpstart his Epic. Selene and Ryan stood by its side for awhile while the motor warmed up. Ryan would return to his farm and she would stay here to help Hirsh deal with phone, furnace and the ten thousand things that needed doing. The driver's door of Ryan's car was open like a sheltering wing. They stood inside it for a final embrace and long kiss. They talked awhile more and then Ryan climbed in and drove away.

V
Arthur

On the ferry home, Ryan's friends looked pale, haggard and worn from their days of struggling with wet wood and broken pipes. Ryan pushed open the door to his house and found it cold and damp but undamaged. He congratulated himself for having thought to drain the pipes and the pump before he'd left. He crumpled up damp newspaper and lay fires in both the wood heater and cook stove, blowing on each fire until the cedar kindling crackled into life and blazed. By evening his house was cozy, warm and dry again, but he missed the extended family in which he had been living. He missed Selene.

Early spring inched slowly on. The soil was still too wet to turn. On warmer nights frogs chanted their chorus to the stars. Some evenings Ryan walked down the road to spend time with friends. Occasionally people dropped by to share wine or a joint. He took his lantern to the beach at midnight to gather oysters and clams at the low tide. He cooked them up the next day to share with whoever came by. He sharpened his chain saw, repaired fences, and cut down the young alders that were encroaching on the field. He topped up his firewood by cutting down a dead alder in the woods above his house and hauling its pieces down in the wheelbarrow. Once again, everything depended upon the red wheelbarrow. He was busy but he still missed Selene and wondered if she missed him; he pondered of what lasting import their time together was. He walked to the store to phone her but Hirsh's line was still disconnected.

The thaw had made it easy to travel again and the restless tribe, packs on their backs, began to move hither and yon. One evening when Ryan was cooking his dinner, he heard a car stop at the corner. He heard the door slam, voices, and then the car moved off down the road. Minutes later the gate slammed followed by footsteps on the porch; then the knock at the door.

He opened it in excitement and found not Selene, but Jean, a former student from his teaching days in the Kootenays, smiling at him from the settling night. They hugged and then held each other at arm's length to have a good look. Gone was the teenager who he had taught several years before. Now, in her place, stood a woman, not much younger than himself, on her own for the first time, making decisions, creating her life. Her green eyes were framed by the ringlets of curly brown hair that hung from beneath her toque. He invited her into his fire-warmed, lamp-lit world.

After dinner they threw a mattress down on the floor. They sat in front of the wood heater, hugging their knees and staring into the fire. Illuminated by the warmth and firelight from the heater's open door, they talked about all the things that had happened since Argenta: her travels and cello studies; his move to the island and the breakup of his marriage.

"Do you remember the night you came down to the party at The Landing?"

Ryan looked into the fire. He remembered his long walk down the road, carrying a pack with his sleeping bag inside in case he couldn't get a ride back that night. He'd started walking the 17 K to The Landing, thinking that a car or truck would come by and give him a ride, but no one had come and he'd had time to walk and think. Earlier in the year, the students had started having parties that they called Love Ins down at The Landing. The school had always been conceived of as a means of bringing income into this remote community and students were boarded with community members. Now the students found that the school's influence and rules were seamless, extending into every home. Its eyes were everywhere. Only The Landing, a beautiful walk down the road above the lake, was beyond its reach. Samara hosted the students and the school was unable to find an acceptable rationale why the students could not stay with her. She was a land owner and the mother of a student in the school. They couldn't find a reason, but they didn't like it.

The more rebellious students turned to The Landing as a place to be out of reach of the school and all its rules. He remembered walking past the old Bulmer place that day, looking down at its house still standing on a little effluvium that extended out into the lake. He remembered hearing the story that Bulmer's wife had "gotten bushed" and was never seen in public again, glimpsed only occasionally as a pale face appearing briefly at the window when someone drove up.

"Yeah, I do. Sheila had left to live in Vancouver and I was alone in the Old Coleman place. You guys never invited us down to the Love Ins because we were staff. I never knew whether it was because you were pissed off with us because we were part of the school or whether it was because you liked us and didn't want to put us in a bind. It was the first time I'd been down. I think everyone felt sorry for me because I was suddenly living alone. All of the students were there and some of the back to the landers that weren't part of the school. I remember this great full moon rising over the mountains. Someone put on The Doors—real loud—and the music was floating through the orchard. We jumped from the barn into piles of hay and played hide and seek in the moonlight under the old apple trees."

Jean turned her head and gave him a shy smile "Yes, but that's not all." She put her hand on his arm. "Remember how you Jane and I all slept together, each in our own sleeping bag? You were in the middle and we snuggled on either side of you like spoons. When one of us turned, we all turned."

"Yeah, it was far out, but I'm a little embarrassed by that. I was a teacher. You and Jane were students. We didn't do anything, but it shouldn't have happened."

"I thought it was cool. You were on faculty but I knew you were more like us. I was awake all night. I remember the moon shining on the snow capped peaks. I remember the sound of the creeks crashing down out of the mountains."

Ryan got up to get more wood for the fire. He went barefoot out the door to bring in an armful of alder. He placed it in the wood heater and poked at it so the flames weren't squelched. Sparks crackled for awhile and swirled like fireflies in the open firebox. Once the fire had calmed down, he came and sat by Jean again.

She gazed into the fire, "It was supposed to be a Quaker school, but it was so un-Quaker. Maybe it was the time, the music. Maybe it was just all of us living together out in the bush at the end of the world. We were so close. Sometimes we'd just sit and stare into each other's eyes. The staff got so paranoid about students sleeping together that they made all these schedules that gave us 20 minutes to get from the school to our home just so that there was no time for anything to happen."

"Yeah, I know. Sheila and I fought that in the meetings, but no one listened. We were seen as too young, too much like the students, to know much. Maybe that was true."

"You know, after I graduated I started reading about the Quakers. I realized that the early ones were into intense love. They believed that we each had an inner light to guide us. Someone, maybe it was John Naylor, rode into Bristol, surrounded by naked followers who scattered blossoms in front of him. Of course he spent the rest of his life in jail, but that doesn't sound like fundamentalism to me. It's like they were so clearly into ecstatic community."

"Yeah, but the school got a lot of its funding from Eastern Quakers who were basically fundamentalists. They sure as hell didn't want any naked ecstasy going on."

"Yeah, but all their prohibition just transformed our feeling for each other into this huge yearning. I think we all loved each other. That's why the three of us slept together that night. I think that, actually, we rediscovered the real meaning of Quakerism, but it freaked out the members of the meeting."

"You got that right. You guys stumbled on the forbidden inner rapture. Bad move. They had pretty well sanitized that out by then." Ryan patted her hand in a consoling "there, there," sort of way.

"Yeah, well it wasn't like any of us were doing anything. They saw to that, but it made the yearning even stronger."

She picked up the arm that she was resting on him and draped it over his shoulder. She rested her head against him. "Maybe I just had a crush on you, but I always wondered what might have been between us, if you hadn't been married and I hadn't been a student." She looked up at him, her eyes seeking his. They sat alone together in the fire-lit cabin, two almost adults. Ryan wondered about Selene, but didn't say anything. It was all too new to know. Ryan put his arm around her.

Slowly, in the midst of all the talk they began to touch each other. Slowly, it turned into love making. They lay back, the firelight flickering on their bodies. Later, when they collapsed into quietude, the fire had died to embers. Ryan pulled a blanket over them and stroked her back. Neither of them slept well that night. Ryan found Selene rattling through his mind. In the morning things felt strange.

Jean sat up and pulled on her shirt and sweater "You know, Ryan, I think I'm just going to catch a ride to the morning ferry, things don't feel right between us somehow."

"Yea, I know, you're right. I'll go with you and drive you to Nanaimo so we can talk on the way."

They gathered up her things, leaving the tangle of covers in front of the cold wood heater, and raced out the door in time to catch the last ride. On the ferry they sat quietly next to each other, sipping coffee from the Styrofoam cups that they had bought at the cafe.

On the way to Nanaimo, when the heater had warmed up the car, Ryan said. "You know, like, what I didn't tell you last night is that I've just met this woman. I didn't really know if it was serious or not, but last night in the middle of, uhh, everything, I realized that I was more connected to her than I thought. Like I didn't understand how connected I was. I didn't know what to do. I guess you must have felt that."

She listened in silence and seemed almost relieved. After a long time she said, "I'm so glad you told me that, it explains some of the strange feelings I've been having." They lapsed into silence, watching the outskirts of Nanaimo spring up around them. At one point Ryan reached over and held her hand. She took it briefly and, after awhile, let it go again. She seemed all right until he dropped her at the ferry. As she was about to close the door, she turned back to him and leaned into the car. "Get better soon," she said and closed the door behind her. Ryan watched her walk into the crowd, becoming just one of the legion of people carrying packs, each in the bloom of their youth, each with too personal a tale to tell.

Rather than drive back to Vasquez, Ryan turned his car south toward Saanich, toward Selene. Hirsh's phone was still dead and Ryan would just have to drop by and see what was happening. In truth, he could hardly wait.

On the long two lane ribbon of highway, the Envoy went faster than Epicly possible. Ryan wondered if Selene still felt a connection to him or whether it had been just a passing thing, a winter romance born of snow and isolation. He knew that a friend from California was coming to visit and that he used to be Selene's boyfriend, several boyfriends back. He didn't know the current nature of their friendship. If Ryan and Selene even had a relationship, it was still in its unformed beginning. He heard Selene's laughter at his situation. The days were still so short that when Ryan arrived at the farm house, its windows were already shining like amber in the gathering darkness. Selene's Minx was parked in the yard.

Ryan bounded up the stairs. As Selene opened the door, the dogs barked and came tumbling out over each other. Selene yelled at them, and grabbed their collars to usher them out, all the while smiling through the chaos at Ryan. Ryan got in the house and shut the door after himself. It was then that he saw Selene's friend sitting at the table, exactly where he had sat on that winter night that now seemed so long ago. Her friend had rusty hair, pale skin and seemed a bit slumped and withdrawn.

When Ryan was fully in and the dogs were fully out—barking and howling on the porch—Selene gave him a hug, a moulding sensual hug and a look that left no doubt about her affection. She introduced him to Arthur. Then they smoked together, the ritual toke that, like the tobacco in Native American ceremonies, brought them together.

Arthur told Ryan the story of his travels. Tomorrow, after getting some money from the bank, he would be returning to California. From time to time Selene filled both their cups from the cracked brown teapot, resting her hand on each of their shoulders as she did so.

When Arthur got up to go to the bathroom, Selene reached both hands across the table and pulled Ryan to her. They kissed in a leaning arch over the kitchen table.

"I have so much to say," Ryan said.

"Me too,"

"Is it ok I'm here?"

"It's great. I'm just wondering if you would mind sleeping in Hirsh's room tonight. He's off somewhere with a new lady. I'd just like not to abandon Arthur this last night. He's been having a hard time. We've really just been holding each other." She gave him a look that was filled with love and trust.

"I could go," Ryan said.

"No, it's not like that, really, I want you, I don't want to miss a minute of you. That is, if it's ok with you. Art and I are really just good friends. I told him about you, that I met a man who I'm excited about. I just don't want to dump him like a hot potato on his last night. He's hurting."

Ryan thought of his visit with Jean. Ryan heard the sincerity that poured from Selene. It seemed like something out of Sir Gawain, a test of love. Ryan decided to let it be.

They sat up smoking, drinking tea and talking. Arthur told him a little about his life. "Yeah, I'm working on a Master's in Archaeology. There's not much left for me in California. My partner's gone. My friends in our communal house, my only real family, have scattered. Maybe I'll come to Canada and start again up here. I hate the way the war is going. In SF we had 300,000 people march down Market Street and nothing changed. Some guy burned himself in protest on the steps of the Department of Justice. The government is so insular. It just doesn't give a shit. It's hopeless. I can't stay in school much longer. If it wasn't for the fucking draft, I wouldn't be there. I gotta do some living, man.

"Everybody is doing this great stuff, starting farms, travelling in craft fairs, making candles, playing music, and I'm still in the library hitting the books. I feel locked into the past, locked into methodology, locked into studying dead fucking cultures. All around me living people are starting their own culture. Man, what a time. How often do we get to start a culture? I mean, intentionally take the elements from other cultures and put them together into a living culture that we think might work; maybe pass it on to our children to see what they'll do with it. It's bigger than an intentional community. There has always been something so

59

precious and elitist about intentional communities. This is an intentional culture. Who knows what will happen. This is amazing and I'm missing it, locked into the past."

They talked into the small hours of the night, squeezing as much living from the day as they could. When it was time to go to bed Ryan went into Hirsh's room. He threw Hirsh's discarded clothes off the bed and climbed in. Lying there, he listened to Selene's and Arthur's voices come across the house from her room. Ryan heard her pad past his door to the bathroom to brush her teeth. There was a little knock at the door and she stuck her head in and then came in and sat on the bed. She was wearing her long cotton gown that both covered and revealed her body. She stroked his arm and then slid under the covers and lay next to him. She curled against him, putting her head on his shoulder and a leg over his torso. Ryan felt the fire that still burned between them. "Thank you," she said, "It means a lot to me. I'll make it up to you." They kissed. She tasted of tooth paste, a mint flavoured kiss.

They lay together a while longer; it felt to Ryan like he had come home. And then she slid out from under the covers and left, swaying seductively as she walked. She looked back at him over her shoulder and, as she closed the door, whispered "tomorrow."

Ryan had never let his heart stay open to a woman that he knew was sleeping with another man; had always backed away in anger. He heard their muffled voices from across the house for awhile, a brief burst of laughter and then the house creaked into silence. Ryan really didn't know if they were lovers or just holding each other. He remembered that he and Selene had technically just held each other for many nights but it was an erotically charged holding. Sexuality seemed to have become ambiguous. People who weren't lovers or who were married to someone else, could hold each other or even sleep next to each other. It was no longer a question of simply being faithful or unfaithful: a huge middle ground had opened up where while not exactly being unfaithful, one wasn't exactly being faithful either. A friend of Ryan's, who's marriage had been hit by The Disintegration, that great wave of experimentation, confusion, wildness, and ecstasy that was tearing everyone apart, now lived alone with her small child at the corner of Howe and Faithful in Victoria. "That was exactly the question," she said. Meanwhile, Ryan vibrated with an erotic charge almost as intense and trance-like as when he and Selene lay together. He thought of tomorrow and finally drifted off in Technicolor dreams.

In the morning Ryan heard Selene rise and run a bath. He could hear her splish-splashing around. Then she came into his room with a towel wrapped around her hair and another around her body. She was warm and flushed from the bath. Ryan peeled back the covers and held his hand out to her. She slipped the towel off her body and slid into bed with him. For just a few minutes they lay entranced in each other's arms. Then she slid out and wrapped the towel around herself again. "Time to make breakfast," she said.

When Ryan dressed and emerged into the kitchen, Selene and Arthur were getting ready to go out.

"Arthur has decided to take us out to breakfast, " said Selene.

They put on their coats, Arthur's long black topcoat that made him look like a figure in mourning, Selene's fringed buckskin cowgirl jacket, Ryan's chequered wool logging shirt. She drove them in her Minx to the International House of Pancakes in Brentwood. Ryan wore his psychedelic Stetson, its domed cubist face grinning its happily fractured grin at the world from above his head. It was great being a hippy in the days when there weren't so many. They created a stir when they walked into the restaurant. Families looked up from their breakfasts; fingers were pointed and parents had whispered conversations with their children: "That's what you don't want to become when you grow up."

The three of them picked a big booth by a window and slid in across the turquoise Naugahyde upholstery. They all sat together on the same side, looking out across the restaurant, Selene with Arthur and Ryan on either side.

VI
The Visit

It was in the fullness of spring, after the blossoms had come and gone and the green-world had re-established itself on earth that Selene packed up her Hillman Minx and drove up island to move in with Ryan. This was not a high commitment activity. She simply carried her three or four boxes and her big frame backpack onto the ferry. Ryan had arranged with his friend Reston to meet her and they drove in his great four wheel drive army surplus invasion vehicle down to the dock. They helped her carry her boxes up the loading ramp and put them in the back of the truck. Then they ground on down the island to the whirr of this great rust-coloured, four wheel drive, insect-shaped vehicle's many gears. Wheels turned within wheels as Reston's gloved hand dextrously and continuously worked the levers.

Over the next few days she arrayed her arrowheads and medicine pouches on Ryan's windowsills. He cleared a shelf for her on the small bookcase in the short passageway that divided his two rooms. On one side of the passageway was the bookcase; on the other, the paned French doors that opened out to the bluff. She arranged her ephemerides and her books on Native American cultures and then stepped back—as far as she could in the narrow passage—to look at them. She seemed to enjoy her little shelf. Ryan showed her how to use the woodstove, where the dry wood was, and where the axes were. She was used to all this from growing up in eastern Oregon. Ryan looked out the window and saw her lean body arching high; the axe about to fall devastatingly on a piece of wood that Ryan knew was truly doomed.

Since Sheila had left, his affairs all had the ambiguity of each person not really knowing what they meant to the other. This was the first time a woman had lived with him since Sheila had left. Ryan and Selene cooked together. After breakfast they went out and turned the soil. At night they looked through his box of seeds and decided what to plant. Selene liked making plans: they drew little diagrams of where this and that would go. She read about the rotation of crops and asked him what was planted in certain places last year and the year before.

They had friends over and cooked for them, or sometimes they walked out at night to eat at Mariel and Reston's or Alexis and Sammies. Sometimes they made the long trip down to Miriam and Isaac's. It was all couples. Couples invited them into the world they shared, the world of contained, plighted, and trothed sexuality. Ryan showed her around. She talked gardens, water supplies and building. If people were interested she drew a chart for them. Ryan was very proud of her, this beautiful quick-witted woman he had brought home with him. He loved seeing his friends warm up to her. He loved seeing the dextrous way that she became part of the island community and began to fit right in.

In the midst of this, their sexuality was wilder than ever. Not having the constraints of jobs or definite timetables, they made love whenever they wanted to. They made love on the little grassy knoll that was hidden behind the house. On warm days, they made love on remote beaches and on the top of bluffs. There were so few people around that this was possible. It was primal and Edenic, like Adam and Eve long ago. Sometimes when friends came clattering into the front yard they caught them flushed and hastily pulling on their clothes. They put up with lots of newlywed jokes.

Ryan was embarrassed but also proud at being caught this way. It was such a change to be in a relationship where sexuality was at the core rather than on the periphery. The tasks were the same as when Sheila lived with him, working in the garden, cutting and stacking wood, preparing food, making shopping lists, cutting down trees and bucking them up, but the fact of their lovemaking made everything different, imbued it with a life that Ryan had never known.

The grass grew brown; maples began to turn yellow; red berries clustered on the Arbutus; the sky was clear and blue for days on end. The garden was for harvesting; the daytime tides were low enough to gather clams and oysters; the waters were warm enough for swimming. Everywhere people were swimming, feasting, harvesting. They were also spending time, some time every day, cutting down trees and bucking them up for firewood. Geese began to fly overhead. Chainsaws echoed in the woods, near and far. By the sea or on the light soaked bluffs people began to hear the woodpecker's cry. Its downward note pierced the air and announced the turn of the season.

Selene and Ryan were still as passionate as ever but a certain friction had entered into their relationship. Ryan began to find her continual planning irritating. She began to be frustrated by his randomness; by the 101 partially completed projects that lay everywhere around the house and farm. Ryan liked to work on all of them at once, crank each one a few notches forward every day. They became just a little cross with each other:

"Why do you always have to plan everything out, why can't you just go with what you feel like doing in the moment?"

"I just wish you'd finish something every now and then. This whole place is a work in progress. I look around, nothing is complete here. Everything needs doing."

But it still felt like summer and they escaped their domestic quandaries by visiting far and wide. The thing about an island is that everybody knows everybody else, at least a little, so Ryan knew almost everybody on the island, at least a little. He was introducing Selene to the whole community, showing her this interesting hive of people. This was so different from the urban anonymity in which they had both spent so much of their lives. Ryan took her, on these late summer days, down the leafy roads filled with woodpecker calls. They traveled a variety of trails and ended up at a variety of cabins, log houses, or plastic shacks.

Plastic Shacks. Since most of the abandoned log houses and shaked cabins had already been taken, newcomers had invented the Plastic Shack. Plastic Shacks were simple pole structures covered with plastic sheeting. They usually had plastic, covered with second hand carpets on the floor; Indian bedspreads were hung on some of the walls for privacy. The rest of the house, including the roof, was like one great blurry window. The construction plastic used to build them was not clear, so it was like living in a giant cataract or an impressionist painting. The light streamed in and outside the forest could be seen as blurry lines vaguely ascending toward the sky.

Selene and Ryan drank tea sitting on carpeted floors at tables made of log rounds. They smoked joints, helped weed lettuce or harvest potatoes from gardens that had been fenced with alder poles and scavenged fish netting. The free-range cattle that wandered around the island had figured out that the newcomer's fences were flimsy at best, and that a few good pushes would yield delicacies like Brussels sprouts and kale. Lost gardens were a frequent topic of conversation. The lesson was that fences were not symbolic structures: they were not there to make the cows think that the area was fenced. As Johnny, an old hermit who read Thoreau and had lived most of his life on the island, put it: "If you don't build a good fence you ain't fooling nobody but yourself."

Sometimes they helped the people they visited to stack wood or cut the wire worms out of carrots in preparation for storage. Selene said that in native cultures people were never idle: they'd spend hours together talking, telling stories and visiting, but would always be lending their hands to something that needed to be done, like rolling iris stalks on their thighs to separate the fibres for rope. Everyone was trying to be more tribal.

Once they had visited the people Ryan knew well, they began dropping in on some of the newer people on the island. Often, just to find someone's trailhead, they had to stop and ask the nearest neighbour. In the absence of phones, people had learned just to accommodate visitors, to stop and have tea or incorporate them into what they were doing.

One day—a portentous phrase full of intimations of things to come—they decided to visit Russ, a man who Ryan had met at the Legion dances and on the ferry. Russ had fixed up a little cabin somewhere near the south end and had invited him to visit. All Ryan knew was that Russ' cabin was on a rocky inlet between the south end's two major bays. It would be an adventure just to find it.

It was on a clear late summer day that Selene and Ryan set out. They caught several rides, and walked for several miles between rides. On the final ride, with Jim and Verna, they climbed out of the back of the truck and joined them for tea at their homestead. There was no hurry. Their days were like that. They were young and full of boundless social energy. They enjoyed visiting several different people a day. For Ryan, having always been a loner, this was fun. Now he knew how it felt to be part of a community. As one of the first newcomers, a founding member, he was also a little puffed up and proud.

After tea and a toke, they started walking down the dusty road again, past old homesteads whose silvered snake fences lay tumbled in the brown grass. Feral sheep raised their heads to look at them. Sometimes the sheep went placidly back to their grazing; other times they ran for the cover of the forest, their dingle berries clacking like lead bells. The sun moved slowly on its arc. Leaves spiraled down out of the late summer trees. Selene and Ryan carried small day packs and stopped at an abandoned orchard to pick some early apples to bring to Russ. In the middle of the orchard was an old house almost entirely mounded over by a climbing vine that ran in and out of its empty windows. The house was almost invisible in the greenery. They stopped to eat juicy apples while around them the crickets sounded like tiny bells announcing autumn.

After several bends in the road, they found the head to Russ' trail. It was really just a place to step off the road, easy to miss without the exact instructions that the people at the last farm had given them. Everyone's life seemed to have some element of hiding.

Selene and Ryan stepped off the road onto the trail, which ran through a sparse forest of arbutus and small second growth fir. They walked in single file, she in the lead. At the coast, the trail turned south, traversing a chain of grassy valleys each of which ran to the sea. Each valley was separated from the next by rocky little ridges. It was really just a sheep trail running up and down along the windswept cliffs. Across the water they could see the low plane of Vancouver Island. Snow-capped Mt. Arrowsmith rose up out of its autumn haze. To the southwest, the plume from the pulp mill at Harmac rose into the sky like a diminutive geyser.

At the top of the last ridge, they looked down into the valley and saw Russ's weathered cabin. It was small, ancient and slump-roofed; perched on a cliff above an inlet. It still had glass windows, a great luxury compared to the flapping plastic stapled over the windows of most reclaimed homes. Its shakes were silvered by the sea. Winter firewood was piled neatly under the eaves.

In front of the cabin was a garden whose picket fence shone with the colour of freshly split cedar. Russ was on his hands and knees weeding and did not see them. Even from this height, they could see the neatly ordered rows of his garden. Ryan, who liked imitating

Ravens, made a raven call to announce their arrival. Russ stood and turned toward them, shading his eyes against the afternoon sun. He did not recognise them, but wiped the dirt off his hands and came through the garden gate to greet them.

He waited where the trail came down off the bluff and, as Selene and Ryan came closer, laughed when he saw who they were.

"Hi man, I'm glad you made it. I couldn't see who you were. The sun was directly behind you and all I could see were these two silhouettes with haloes of light for hair. You looked like a couple a spiritual beings coming down the trail. "

They all laughed. He gave Ryan one of those hippy handshakes where the thumbs intertwine. His face was in a broad grin. He was unusually clean cut for an islander, his light brown beard neatly trimmed, his almost blond hair short and well cut. He turned to Selene and kind of nodded and grinned at her. He didn't say anything, nor did she.

"Russ this is Selene, Selene, Russ,"

"Hi!"

"Hi!"

They smiled at each other a moment and then Russ turned.

"Come and see the 'ol place. I was just going to take a break."

They caught up and walked with him across the grassy, sheep-grazed valley bottom, past the bright wood of the pickets, past the firewood stacked under the eaves, to the side of the cabin where the door was.

Ryan had felt something pass between Selene and Russ when they met, and some kind of fear or jealousy arose within him. He suddenly understood that travelling the island, showing her off like this, especially to the young bachelors, was dangerous. Better to stay home, repair fences and turn soil; better to let her be the oppressed country wife, at home working while Ryan traveled around, but it was too late for that. Russ pushed the door open and stood aside, gesturing for Selene and Ryan to enter. They walked into his ordered world, a small room in which everything was neatly stacked, piled or folded. There was an enormous big paned, wavy glassed window looking out over the rocky cove. In front of it was a narrow bed that was neatly made, with cushions placed against the window sills so it could be used as a couch during the day. Russ had avoided the usual bachelor miasma of tools and disassembled chainsaws stacked on every available surface. Even the dishes had been washed and were stacked in a drainer on his little plywood sink board.

Russ pumped a polished brass kerosene burner and poured water from a bucket into the kettle.

"Where's your water from?" Selene asked the standard question.

"There's an old well over by the apple trees. I had to clean it out but it has good cold water now."

The floors were neatly swept; the broom was leaned behind the door. Outside the window—whoever had built this shack knew about light and view—the sea luminesced in the late afternoon sun, marking time with its lapping swell on the rocks below.

Russ went out to the well and pulled up a sealed plastic bucket. He pried off the lid and took out a block of cheese in a plastic bag. He came back to the cabin with it and cut thin slices off the block and served them on a plate with pieces of hard tack, the kind that came in big circles with a hole in the middle. They sipped tea and snacked on hard tack and cheese.

" Yea, I got the cheese at Save-On-Meats. They also sell polish sausage and other greasy delicacies. They're also the only butcher shop in Vancouver that still sells horsemeat."

"You ever try it?" Selene said, talking through the food in her mouth.

"Naw, but I like the cheeses and sausage. The price is right. Sometimes the cheese has a bit of mould on the outside, but once you cut it off, it seems to be fine."

Russ passed around a small pipe carved in the shape of a whale. The blowhole was the bowl; the tail the stem. They each took one toke. Stoned, it became all too apparent to Ryan that there was chemistry, magnetism, between Selene and Russ. Their eyes and conversation connected and intertwined. He entered her with his words, his stories, his glance, and she opened for him, letting him in with her laughter and the languor of her body. She had draped herself in his one chair, a canvas hammocky kind of thing on a wrought iron frame. Ryan was included only with a kind of perfunctoriness. He was the witness.

After awhile Ryan began to feel hurt and angry. He said "I think I'll go out and have a look around." He hoped Selene would follow him, out of some kind of loyalty, but she and Russ merely smiled up at him and looked accepting. "Sure." They both said.

Ryan walked out the door into the benevolent afternoon sunlight and out to the edge of the sea. Russ' boat was pulled up high on the beach below. It was tied with a line to a big boulder, its small outboard tilted up off the beach. Ryan walked out to the point where he could see down to the island's end. Past the last point there was open blue sea and the distant haze of

Vancouver. He turned around and realised that on his left were the cliffs that he had seen in a dream that he had been given when he first came to Vasquez. Just like that, the dream came back to him.

In it Ryan had been cast up on a far-away island. He had climbed out of the sea onto its beautiful forested shores. On the island there was a tribe of beautiful golden people who wore no clothes, who wore only beautiful golden rings around their necks, around their arms, around their ankles. Golden rings dangled from their ears and from the septum of their noses. They were very tanned and lean. They sang as they worked in the fields, sang as they carried their bundles up the road. They walked in step, in long dancing lines that undulated through their journey. Life was a dance. They didn't make art, they were art. Their life was their art. They left nothing behind but the gold rings they wore. When their time came, in the fullness of their eternal youth, they simply lay down on the ground and died. Every day their friends came and placed offerings—flowers, boughs, sheaves of grain, the first fruit of every crop—on their bodies. This went on year after year until a hill was born and a great spreading fruit tree grew out of it. Sheep grazed beneath it. A village arose out of their body.

They had welcomed him into their tribe. They gave him a neck ring of woven reeds to start with. They told him that, once, all their rings were just woven reeds; and that Ryan would have to turn his to gold.

In the dream Ryan lived with them for many years but his ring did not become gold. It became golden reeds but Ryan could see that the fibres of the reeds were still intact beneath a thin leaf of gold. In every other way Ryan was like them. He wore no clothes. He grew brown in the sun, and muscled and lean from the daily work. He slept with the beautiful women. There were no marriages. No one questioned where a child came from. Each child was welcomed from its mother's womb and given a tiny necklace of reeds. They all raised the children.

One day, his reed necklace fell off. The delicate gold leaf blew away like chaff in the wind. All Ryan held in his hand were dried-up untransformed reeds. They were as they always were, but worn-out and old. Ryan ran to a creek and looked at himself in a still pool. There were no mirrors here. They were each other's mirrors. The whole tribe was their mirror. Ryan had not seen himself for many years. He looked into the pond and saw, beyond the tiny ripples made by the water skeeters, that he had gone grey; that he was not ageless; that he would not be able to simply lie down in the beauty of his youth and start a village. Time was ticking at his back. Ryan had not turned his neck ring into gold. He clutched at his handful of tattered reeds.

He returned to the village to seek succour, but they were angry with him. They pointed at his missing necklace. The women he had slept with covered their eyes and ran into their gracious grass houses. They tried not to see the grey in his hair, the wrinkles on his cheeks. He had brought death and corruption among them.

Suddenly he was running. The men were driving him off, driving him back into the sea from whence he had come. At every turn they appeared in front of him blocking his way. They were herding him to the islands edge, moving in long sinuous lines, connecting with each other, linking up, forming a long dancing net that closed in around him. He ran along the cliffs and just when he was about to jump, he saw two ordinary looking men in a rowboat waving frantically to him. It was as though they had been waiting for him. They gesticulated to a point ahead of him and motioned for him to run. The tribal net was now alive with frightening chants. It was rapidly closing around him. Going to where the men in the boat pointed, Ryan saw a small trail going down between the cliffs. He ran down to the beach, and naked, having dropped the reed collar, ran into the sea and started swimming toward the boat. It was summer in the dream and the waves were September warm. He looked back and all around him on the cliffs the men of the tribe were waving and chanting. Some had begun to descend the trail after him. When they reached the beach they gesticulated and threw stones at him.

The boat rowed toward him and pulled him naked aboard. The men were dressed in homey clothes, faded jeans and flannel shirts. They were grizzled with weathered lines on their faces. They threw a blanket over him as Ryan shivered in the bow of the boat. They turned and rowed diagonally away from the shore, using the wind at their back to help get beyond the rocks and spears that were being hurled at them. Tribal men followed all along the cliff tops, hurling spears and chanting. When the island's natives realised they couldn't catch them, they started a long moaning line dance that followed the boat, undulating along the shore. Ryan could see their brown bodies and their golden rings. They were full of life force, full of the energy of the sun. Even in war their penises were proudly erect.

As they danced they became transparent, like jelly fish or glass shrimp. Ryan could see every detail of them, see through them. Their erections were transparent too, giant glass tools. He could see every organ pulsing and beating within them, he could see the food moving slowly down through their convoluted tubes, he could see, their blood circulating. By some trick of dream vision, he could even see the individual blood cells coursing through their engorged penises.

The oarsman turned away from the island and started the long voyage back to what looked like the distant shores of Vancouver Island. The transparent beings remained on the island, dancing and chanting at the top of the cliffs. Slowly, very slowly, they became more and more diaphanous and evanescent. Finally they became bright spots of light, like sun dogs moving on the cliff tops and then Ryan couldn't see them anymore. The island was quiet and forested like the day he had swum ashore. It was just an island, a dark forested spot on the horizon that he watched while it faded out of view. He tightened his blanket around him and surrendered to the rocking of the boat. He was shivering.

Ryan had awoken from the dream sweating and trembling in his dark little cabin. His wet sleeping bag was bunched around him. The night had been absolutely dark and silent. He had lain in the dark and played these images over and over in his head until dawn, and thought about the story they told.

He hadn't told Selene the dream yet. He kept it to himself, as part of his interior landscape, in the chest of maps and diagrams that he carried around inside his head. Some drawers in this chest were filled with diagrams of cars, of chainsaws, of how to build houses, of how to prune trees. In other drawers there were these vivid medieval illustrations of dreams and visions that he usually didn't know how to interpret. He remembered reading that Hillel had said that a dream not interpreted was like a letter unread. Every now and then he took his dreams out from the dream drawer, unfolded them and admired the vivid art work, the way the stars were painted in gold relief and the bodies of the women were so sanctified and queenly. Now he took this one out to look at again, as he would take it out many times over the course of his life. He looked around. Yes, this was the place where he had seen the tribe travelling along the cliffs, transparent and hurling their spears as he had escaped by boat. He was sure of that. What did the dream mean? Why had it come back today? What did this place mean? He refolded the dream and put it back again.

On his way back to the cabin he walked past the window. He waved at Selene and Russ and they waved back at him. Even from out here he could see the intensity of their contact. The shadows of the scrub juniper were spreading across the clearing. Everything was twisted and sculpted by the wind. Looking around, it was easy to believe in fate, in invisible forces that shaped everything, twisted things from their genetic program. He walked back into the cabin. Selene smiled at him "Russ has invited us for dinner."

The last thing that he wanted to do was to be a captive witness to this conversational lovemaking for another three hours. He was usually easy going and went with the flow (go with the flow, ride with the tide, suck with the muck). But today he was angry and did not feel that way.

"I think I'd rather be heading home while there is still some chance of getting a ride," he said mildly, "it's a long way."

Selene and Russ exchanged a glance. Selene said, "Oh, all right, but I think I'd like to stay awhile, if that's OK with you."

Ryan felt on the spot. It was like she had tossed down a gauntlet. What was Ryan going to say, in front of Russ: "No that's not OK, I'm a jealous, possessive, insecure guy. I want you to come home with me. I feel threatened by Russ, who is so tidy, together and industrious, everything you complain about me not being?"

He did not say that. He kind of nodded, as if in thought—which he was—and said slowly, "yeah I guess." He should have known, since she hadn't come out with him when he wanted to walk, that this wouldn't work. He had assumed that when it came to leaving, since they had come together, that the old rules, the rules that Sheila and he had lived by in their dead marriage, the implicit understandings of coupledom, would work.

Selene rose. "Well, I'll walk you part way to the road." She pulled her lovely long body up out of the canvas chair and pulled her light sweater on over her head. Russ stood up too. When they were all outside, she took his hand. Ryan felt relieved at her taking his hand, saw it as an acknowledgement of their relationship, a showing to Russ that he was her man. She looked back at Russ and smiled, "I'll see you in a little while."

"I'll start the woodstove."

Russ and Ryan simply nodded at each other and said goodbye. They were both smiling. On the trail up the bluff, Selene and Ryan were silent. "Are you pissed off at me?" she finally asked.

"It felt like there was so much happening between you and Russ. I felt uncomfortable. I wanted to break it up. I wanted you to come and walk with me."

"I know," she said, "that's partly why I stayed. I felt you were trying to power trip me. It didn't feel right, like you were putting rules on me. There was a lot happening; it was a powerful connection; I wanted to stay."

Ryan felt angry, but had to acknowledge to himself that that was exactly what he had been doing, being the hurt little boy and hoping that she would follow him out to comfort him. He was angry and ashamed. All his bluster and big man on the island stuff was gone and he felt helpless, insecure, unworthy.

He sat down on a shelf of moss covered rock and she sat next to him. They looked out at the sun lowering itself into the yellow haze over Georgia Strait and Vancouver Island. She sensed his pain and took his hand. They leaned against each other in silence for awhile.

"This is always hard," she said, "but it happens, it happens to everybody if they are honest. It's just part of living. When it happens all our old tapes come up, all the old rules, and tell us not to live, to shut it all down. I really would like to get to know Russ and have dinner with him. You can stay with me. Do you want to come back and say you changed your mind?" This was not true to himself, it was the last thing he wanted, to hang-in out of jealousy, the little witness watch dog. Also there was the question of pride. He shook his head and crumpled up his mouth in distasteful "no."

"Well, I'll come back with you if you want me to, I just have to go back and tell Russ I've changed my mind and say goodbye." She started to stand up but Ryan pulled her back down beside him.

The sun was sinking lower and lower over the horizon and they watched it for awhile. What did he want? On one level he wanted her to come back, to rein her in and clip her wings. She was willing, really, to come back if he wanted her to. But was that right? Could he ask that? He looked at her. She smiled at him like she understood his dilemma, a loving and compassionate smile with just a bit of laughter in it.

Ryan shifted the focus to her. "Well, what do you want?"

"I would like to have dinner with Russ but I don't want to hurt you. I can have dinner with him some other time. If you want me to leave with you, I will. Just say it."

"Some other time." It was like fate pounding on the door. If not now, then later. She would just walk down the road on her own. It was like this experience was in store for him one way or another.

Ryan wanted to be bigger than all that. He desperately wanted her to come home with him, but he didn't want it to be at his command. He couldn't own the hurt, insecure, jealous part of himself, give it the validity that it would need to assert itself and make the command. "How will you get home," he asked.

"There is a moon tonight. The roads are beautiful in moonlight. I can find my way."

"Well, whatever you want," Ryan said.

"Well, then I'd like to stay, but I want that to be OK with you. Otherwise you should come back or we both should go."

Free will. Choice. It was up to him.

"No. you stay if that's what you want."

Her eyes melted as she looked at him. "Are you sure?"

"Yeah, as sure as I can be."

She kissed him deeply. "Thank you," she whispered, "there aren't too many people who would be so understanding of me, so accepting of who I am. It means so much."

She walked all the way to the road with him. Red light from the setting sun fell on her hair through the branches of pine and arbutus. Her hair was tied with a plait of reeds from a pond that they had passed on their way down the island. In the mottled light she looked like she had stepped out of a Pre-Raphaelite painting. At the road they kissed goodbye. "See you later," she said and walked back into the sunset groves, into the dappled darkness of the forest.

VII
The Lake

He began his long walk back up the evening road, past abandoned orchards ringing with crickets. At Jim and Verna's, smoke was already pouring out their chimney. Inside the adults were beginning to cook dinner. No doubt, he thought, struggling with questions of identity and relationship. Outside, their children were still playing under the trees. He kept walking, not wanting to be invited in for dinner.

The children saw him and ran up to the fence.

"Where are you going?"

"Home."

"Where d'you live."

"Ryan's corner."

That's what everybody called it now, except for the old-timers who still called it Geddes' corner and the even older timers, the elite old timers, who called it Walsh's corner. There was a status of seniority in the name you called it, or maybe just an indication of how far in the past, in denial, you were living.

"Oh," one of the children said, unaware of these nuances, "I have a new Barbie doll."

"Hey, that's great."

"She has a boyfriend named Ken. They're going to get married."

How do you know?"

"Because they are."

"OK, bye."

He didn't say (though he wanted to) "I have a girlfriend named Selene and I don't have a clue what we're going to do."

They watched with solemn eyes as he went up the road and disappeared around the bend into the forest. Once or twice, when the truck hadn't been running, they had needed to walk the whole way, sometimes carried on the shoulders of their weary parents. They knew that he had a long road ahead of him.

It was almost dark when he got home. He didn't think she would really come home that night, walk the long road by moonlight, but he had his hopes. He thought she would drink berry wine and lie with Russ on the narrow bed by the big window overlooking the inlet. The brief euphoria of their open conversation and their parting kisses had long since worn off. He was in a turmoil of anger against her. He thought of harsh words to say to her when she came in the door. There were also fantasies of fighting Russ or humiliating him. Surprisingly violent images. And also erotic tension, stoked by unbidden images of Selene languorously opening to him as the moon poured in the window by the sea.

He didn't bother to light the cook stove but took some leftover salmon out of the cooler. He picked lettuce with a flashlight and made a small salad. Then he took his chair outside and ate while he watched the stars emerge in the gathering darkness. The sky began to glow, and then a great moon slowly rose from behind the black tips of the fir trees. He imagined that the little people kept it lashed down during the day, and now they had released it, jumping for joy at the sight of it floating up like a luminous balloon; then racing across the forest floor to catch it.

His fantasy only distracted him for a few minutes. It was not like day, when he could focus his mind by weeding, repairing, cutting wood, mending fences. He struggled to find a place of peace and acceptance, to not give in to the animal furies, the jealousy, the feelings of inadequacy, the desire, all the stuff of tragic arias that raged within him.

He tried to be different, to be in a new way. In the new garden it was jealousy that was the sin, the worm in the rose, not love or passion. He consoled himself that this was just the pain of evolution, of trying to transcend the old human mould by not acting it out.

When he went to bed, he was kept awake by Selene's scent on the sheets and by his own erotic images. The moon passed overhead and the clearing was loud with crickets. Finally, he passed out in the midst of his arousal and slept.

Vaguely, in moments of wakening, he was aware of an owl moving in a great circle through the forest around him. Each time he woke, he heard its rhythmic hoot, WHO, WHO, WHO, WHOHA, HAHOOO come from a different compass point. To his sleepy mind there was magic in this great circle that was slowly being woven around him in the night.

Late at night, he was awakened by the door opening. The moon had finished its course and the night had relapsed into total darkness. Perhaps the little people had lassoed the moon from a tree top and pulled it back down into captivity until tomorrow night's game. At any rate, it was pitch dark, the dark before dawn. The cold dew had stilled the crickets and there was complete silence. He heard Selene slip off her clothes and put them on the chair beside the bed. She was always so tidy. She would never have thought of just throwing her clothes on the floor. She slipped silently into bed.

He turned toward her, wondering if she would turn away from him, but she opened her arms to him and more than met him. They did not speak, and he did not indulge in questions, or she in answers. What was between them was much too urgent for that. It was an act of surrender, of accepting what was, of opening to eroticism. There was no pretence, just her naked presence, alive and open beside him. They lay for hours in primordial wetness, their tongues connected lightly at the tip, their movement minimal. They moved in and out of their bodies, in and out of wakefulness and sleep. In whispers they shared some dreams. They moved into the morning sunshine, threw off the covers and lay with the sun's golden light warming their young bodies. Once more they came together, like overflowing vessels, and let the forces of nature move through them.

It was only late that they got up and made coffee. They were too wiped out to think of doing much that day, but they were in good spirits. They laughed and enjoyed each other's company. For the present, his anger at her was gone, washed away by the night's powerful melding. They watered the garden and packed small packs to go to the lake: to swim, to eat blackberries, to lie in the afternoon sun. She wore almost nothing—shorts, and a thin tank top. Her brown skin glowed in the autumn sun.

At the lake they took off their clothes and sat naked on a grassy hill that slanted into the sun. Little by little others trickled in, single people, couples, families with children, all refugees from the heat and dust of their small farms. They took off their clothes and sat in the dappled shade of the old apple trees. They ate apples from the trees and picked blackberries from the vines at the clearing's edge. They shared simple food: bread and cheese, left over brown rice, carrots from the garden, a chunk of salmon. Someone brought a bottle of home-made wine. Someone else passed a joint around.

He looked around and saw a re-creation of the paradise panel from Bosh's Garden of Earthly Delights: the nakedness, the slim European bodies reaching up to pick fruit that dangled from the bounteous trees. Naked, they returned to their archetypes: the blonds and red-heads looked like they had escaped from canvases by Breugel or Bosh; the darker types, like himself, seemed to have wandered in from the Italian renaissance. There was openness, a lack of shame, amazing peace and harmony.

When it got too hot, they walked naked through the small alders to the edge of the lake. A great old fir had fallen into it, and they walked out on its trunk, past the margin of reeds, and dove into the cool clean water. They played games on the log, wrestled each other and fell in with great splashes and shouts. They floated on their backs and watched the few clouds that drifted by in the sky. The children bobbed around them in their life jackets and inner tubes, splashing and shouting. For this moment it was a song of innocence, Eden, the world before—or after—guilt, shame, and vengeance had had their time.

And, just for today, the angel did not come with his flaming sword. Just for today, their gardens, their failures, their poverty, their conflicts, their addictions, the burdens of life, seemed so far away. It was as if— just for today—the angel had unlocked the gate, taken off the great chain and padlock put there by the crotchety landlord when he had evicted their forebears. For what? Eating apples? Knowing too much? Having sex? No one, over the centuries, had really been able to figure it out.

The angel looked at his watch and let them in for a visit. They wandered in amazement through the ancestral home they had never seen before. They savoured this rare chance, this rare autumn afternoon, where it felt like the weight of the world had been lifted from their backs, and the original sin—whatever it might have been—had been forgiven.

VIII
The Nomad's Tent.

For awhile, for a few days, a week, things went well with Selene and Ryan. They floated on their cloud of love, worked together in their cloud of love, visited around in their cloud of love. But then Ryan felt her begin to go away again; to be less connected; to put out less light like a waning moon. The bristliness returned, the small irritations at each other's ways. They say even love birds will peck each other to death if kept in too small a cage. One day she packed her small pack with a change of clothes and said she was going to visit Russ. "I will be back tomorrow."

Though Ryan was mostly able to contain his feelings, the cloud was now breaking into raindrops and lightning. There was no pretence of her coming back tonight. Tonight was for Ryan alone. He walked her to the corner and they parted with a somewhat perfunctory hug. Ryan watched her walk down the road. It was still the end of Indian summer and she wore shorts and a T-shirt. When she was at the bottom of the hill, a truck blew by him. He watched it stop for her, watched her climb in the back with its other passengers. There was a final wave as the truck disappeared through the tunnel of trees and over the hill into the forest.

The first night was all right. Ryan knew this was coming and had prepared himself for it. She was all around him, her clothes, her books, her pictures, her arrowheads. He had most of her. He wondered about this rhythm of intensity and then the gradual fading into distance.

The next day he worked around the farm, listening for cars on the road, awaiting her arrival and hoping that they would still be together. He feared that if he objected, she would just move in with Russ and that would be the last of her.

Night came, but she did not. Darkness fell over his cabin and she was still not there. He worried about her. He was angry: "You told me..." He wanted to walk down the road, to knock on the door, drag her out, bring her home, but he knew that even if he left now he wouldn't even arrive until midnight. His pride forbade it, so he sought spiritual refuge. There was a theory that if you were really in the here and now, polygamy shouldn't bother you; that when your lover was gone, you would be content in your own space, sufficient in the present moment. This was not nearly how it was for him. He was both tormented and tantalised by unbidden erotic visions of her and Russ as the night passed slowly overhead. His mind, instead of quieting, ran rampant.

The next day she arrived about eleven, her face illuminated, her step light and breezy. She wore her change of clothes. She came to him immediately.

"I'm so sorry, I just couldn't leave last night. It wasn't complete. We were in a process. It would have been brutal just to leave. I knew you'd be worried. I just had to hope you could handle it." She moulded herself against him and took refuge in the curve of his arms, like a weary child. "Would you like me to help you"—he was harvesting tomatoes—"or can we just spend some time together and get connected again?"

They took a blanket, some food, and hiked up the long incline to the bluff that was hidden in the trees above the house. They sat at the top of their world together, looking out over the forest and ocean. They ate lunch and had a toke. He wanted to be mad at her and set limits, say what was all right and what was not, but he was so happy to be with her and so erotically charged that this idea went out the non-existent window. She took off her blouse to gather the sun on her body. When he reached for her she slid easily into his arms. It was as though the last two days away had meant nothing.

These renewals were based on the cloud of love. They were based on the gardens that spread around them. They were based on working together in harmony on the land. They lasted for awhile. And then the intensity faded. They became cross with each other again as their different approach to everything started to aggravate them. They would quarrel. He felt her fade out and begin to go away. She walked down the road.

One day they argued about the zucchini and he asserted himself. He was going to do it his way. The vibes were unpleasant, and for awhile they walked around in stony silence like mechanical zombies doing the various things that need doing in the garden. After awhile she put her gloves down on one of the grassy trails that defined the various plots in the garden and went up to the house. A few minutes later he saw her leave wearing a light jacket. She walked out the gate. At the corner she turned north, not in the direction of Russ's.

That night she didn't return. He was restless, puzzling about what was happening, listening out the window for cars, waiting for her footsteps. He had no idea where at the north end she might be staying. It could be with anyone. He convinced himself that she probably had gone to a gathering or a party and had just stayed when it got too late. He went through anger, indignation, and finally remorse for having been so high handed. When she did come back, in the middle of the next morning, he was shaken and simply asked where she had been. She said she spent the night with Henry, a single man that they both knew. Henry had come to the island with his wife, but all too soon The Disintegration had hit and they split up. She said she had just gone to visit, to see the baby goats he had told her about the last time they met. One thing had led to another.

She approached him cautiously, like you would approach a cornered animal. He was all angles, backing away from her in hurt and anger. She took his arm lightly. "I am sorry I got so riled up, I really am, that's one of the reasons I left, to cool down. Let's be friends." Her hand on his arm, her touch, had a deadly effect on his resolve. She slid into him like a boat into its slip. His anger, yesterday's fight, her disappearance, her spending the night with another man were all washed away on a wave of relief and eroticism that arose like a magnetic field between them. It was as though neither of them could resist or say no. All that was left was to surrender to the force between them. They were held together by it despite whatever else was happening.

He thought of this force as the wild erotic, commonly called "untamed," or "unbridled," but usually only approximated, and then quickly reined back in.

There were always rules; just enough of the wild erotic was let out to keep sex interesting; then it was quickly stuffed back in. He remembered when he was in college going to see a friend perform in Aristophanes' *The Birds*. In the play, Dionysus had broken free and ruled in a little pastoral valley. It started with groups of houris following and worshipping him, the enlivening of everybody, and ended with chaos and murder. The old gods had been lashed down and for good reason, he thought. They would play with us; turn everything topsy-turvy. We must keep them as slaves for our pleasure, keep them on long ankle chains so they didn't ruin our families, our societies, our rules of succession. Yes, by all means, let the gods and goddesses out for a little romp every now and then, but be sure to return them to their cages with prods and lashes.

He wondered if there ever really were priestesses who gave themselves on the temple steps and were honoured and revered for it. Were there ever Babylonian house wives who were welcomed home by a loving husband after their service to the goddess at the temple, after giving themselves to the dusty stranger, the passing carpenter, the miller smelling of flour, the farmer with his hands stained green from the young wheat? Were there maidens who anointed and washed them? Acolytes who bathed and cleansed the men who came to worship?

101

He thought of today's whores, addicted and fallen down in the streets, and wondered where the wild divinity of sex was today? What about the time when people bowed to it as the life force, he asked himself, when we copulated to bring fertility to the fields or to simply honour the urge, the wild god and goddess? He wondered if in this hidden place, far from classical columns and bas-relief chariots, under the influence of rebellion and drugs, the old gods had gotten loose and were having their way with them. How far back to the land did they really want to go, he asked himself.

He did not challenge Selene's freedom. Really, he could not. Her pull was too strong. He needed to have her. He needed to play his part. She glowed with electricity. He could practically see her holding two snakes aloft to heaven, the electrical energies of heaven and earth. Sex was a sacred rite. She was not broken or addicted but walked proudly, with feline gate, on the trails that linked the old homesteads.

But for him there was also his anger, his shame at being with a woman who was unfaithful. There were all the old messages of his father, his mother, all the divorces of past history, the broken walls of Troy, the shame of people talking about him: the cuckold, the man who couldn't keep his woman in line, couldn't keep her satisfied. There was a huge drama, a battle played out in his mind in which the experience of divine freedom was pitched against the constraints of conventional morality and animal jealousy. It was tearing him apart.

After their repeated honeymoons, he went increasingly into anger, seething internal anger at her infidelities. He was surprised at some of the men she chose to sleep with. It seemed to him if she loved him how could she also love this person or that? She simply said, "Everybody has their own beauty, their own power if you take them on their own terms." His ego, his sense of himself as special or different was badly mauled. His animal self bristled. The hair on the back of his neck stood up when he came into the vicinity of another man with whom he knew she had been. She came and went; she was with him less now, but always returned. "Many people want just sex from me. It is important that there is someone who can really love me for who I am," she said, "What you don't understand is that I need you as much as you need me; I can't be me without you being you."

They fought more. He could not disguise his anger at her. She left at the first sign of one of his tirades, went to heaven knows where. At last he could no longer take it. People were gossiping about him. He was full of shame. All this had gone too far. He told her she must make the choice, to live with him as a couple or to move out.

"I can't go back," she simply said, "I can't go back to what we had before."

It was decided, then. She would become her own person. They would dissolve their coupledom. She would build a small house down on the margin of his lower field, down under the trees. It seemed natural enough; everybody who had land was sharing it, letting other people live on it. Far back in the forest was a handmade house built by a man named Mike who Ryan had invited to build on his land several years before. Mike's house was built of boards he had milled himself with his chainsaw.

It was a hot day, a sunny day, when she and he went hand in hand down into the trees to find a site together. They both seemed filled with relief and also sadness. It was cool in the trees, pleasant on this late summer day. She picked a spot under an old fir tree near the edge of the clearing where some warming sun came in. They cleared a spot for the house, digging out the ferns and salmon berries, smoothing the forest loam. "I don't want you to build it for me," she said, "I want this to be my own thing. You can help, but I want to muster my own resources."

It seemed to him that the community, his friends and hers, gave a collective sigh of relief when they announced their separation. The "unnaturalness" of their relationship had been preying on them. A stream of people came to help her build her little house. She mostly stayed at his place and got up in the morning and went down to the site. People came and helped her cut small trees, limb them, and peel the poles.

It was only days until the pole framework went up. It was attached to the old fir tree that became the main upright of the house. Sometimes, at the end of the day, she went home with a friend who had come to help her. She always came to say goodbye to Ryan on these occasions, usually on the pretext of returning some tool that she had borrowed. She let him know where she would be. She gave him a goodbye hug.

Sometimes he would go down to help. Often several of her friends came from various corners of the island to put in a day's work. The late autumn days were still hot and they worked with their shirts off, climbing ladders to nail the framework of poles into place. Everybody seemed to come to put on the plastic skin: to unroll the billowing cloudy plastic from its hardware store roll, to spread it, staple it to the poles and batten it down. Ryan helped too.

When the house was complete, Russ came from the south end with his chain saw and cut a small cedar tree into a hundred and eight thin rounds. Russ and Selene split them into hexagons by splitting the round edges off with an axe. Selene meticulously fit them like tile to make a fragrant floor of hexagonal cedar rounds. She filled the spaces between them with the sawdust from the sawing. She draped a few madras curtains from the walls for privacy. The whole thing was very airy and felt like a nomad's tent or a druid temple. There were little pedestals, cut from the trunks of trees and roughly shaped with a chain saw, placed at different heights around the house to hold candles and lamps. The great trunk of the fir tree was the north wall and the whole house funneled out from the tree, opened and rose to gather heat from the sun-lit south wall. A few old rugs that people had donated went over some of the hexagonal log tiles and completed the yurt-like feeling.

She went over to the mainland—the "other side"—for a single sheet of plywood with which to make a small counter and a large low bed. Henry came from the north end to help her set up her bed on log rounds that he cut with his chain saw. He and she also built the kitchen counter out of poles and the remainder of the plywood. She came to Ryan's house and gathered her few things, her arrowheads, her bundles of herbs and pouches, and said goodbye to him with a shy smile. He watched her walk through the long grasses of the field. Halfway to her house she stooped to pick up something that she had dropped and continued on her way.

On that night she initiated her house by inviting Henry to stay with her. Later she told Ryan that she had cooked a simple one-pot meal for them on her primus stove: brown rice with oysters and some greens. She cooked the rice and at the last minute had put in the greens and oysters on top of it to steam. Two white enamel dish pans from the other side had served as a sink. Her simple kitchen had worked alright.

Late that, night from the terrace outside his house, he could see the faint glimmer of candle light through the trees at the margin of the forest. He dared not go closer.

IX
First Snow

In truth, even though she now had her own house, Selene and Ryan had not separated completely. Sometimes she came up at dusk, the late autumn dusk of six pm, when he was cooking dinner, and he invited her to stay. He had become another of her lovers. Sometimes she came by with a bag of food from the store and told him what she was making, and asked whether he would like to come down. He spent the odd night with her in her candle lit temple. One morning she got up and started her little kerosene stove while he was still in bed. She brought him coffee, dark chocolate and herself, breasts provocatively exposed, as she set the tray down on the pedestal beside the bed.

She was gone too, for days at time, spending time with her new lover at the Valley House, travelling to the south island to visit Russ. Having her own place had only expanded the range of her adventures. Sometimes while he was putting in fence posts or splitting wood he saw one of her lovers cross the lower field and slip down the trail to her house in the forest.

Selene and he began to spend much less time together, but the time that they did spend was intense and sexual. Now that he didn't "own" her, now that she was officially not "his," there was not so much shame about being another of her handful of lovers. Selene and Ryan also liked to talk. They would sit on top of the bluff and listen to the ravens tell their story; puzzle about the code of squawks, hoots and clicks that the birds relayed down the island; wonder what the birds were saying. They liked to walk naked on the bluffs, where nobody ever came, and make love spontaneously on the carpet of moss with the warm autumn sky above them, or in the shade of the small pine trees that grew on the bluff. These were the last precious warm days. Sometimes they sat hand in hand and watched the deep blue currents that swirled around the island or the gusts of wind spread across the surface of the sea. "Sometimes I feel we are married," she said, "spiritually I mean, more bonded than most people despite everything, despite that we live separately now, despite the freedom I enjoy. I've never said this to anyone else."

They still did tarot readings by lamp light at his place or hers. One night the Devil card came up in both of their readings. It showed a great leathern winged figure sitting on a throne. It was definitely hermaphroditic, with the horns, hairiness and musculature of a man but the breasts of a woman. "Ah… the devil can give nourishment," said Selene.

Chained to The Devil's throne and on fire, sharing the fire of the torch that the devil held, were a naked man and woman. They wore garlands that seemed glazed with fire. They had tails: hers tipped with a cluster of fruit, his with a leaf of flame.

"They are on fire," he said. He looked at the card for a long time. The woman's body was long and slim, like the bodies in medieval woodcuts, like Selene's body.

Selene said "What else do you see?" He looked for a long time. He didn't see anything. Selene brought the lamp closer. "Look at the chains around their necks," she said, "what do you see about them?"

"The links are really big."

"What else?

"I don't know, what?"

"Look at the size of the loops. The chains are hanging around their necks in big loops."

He saw that the chains were not tight around each of their necks. "Oh yeah, what about it?"

Selene looked at him and smiled. She took his hand. "It would be easy enough just to slip them off if they wanted to. There is really nothing holding them. The chains are a pleasant fiction. The man and woman are really there because they want to be. They like to be on fire."

Autumn came with rain and wind that shook her little plastic house. The small tin heater did not put out enough heat to make it a space of warmth and comfort. The roof dripped. She started spending a lot of time at Ryan's house and at some of the other single men's houses. He did not want to invite her back for the winter.

"I can't go back either," he said. It didn't seem that many of the people she was seeing wanted to invite her in for the winter either. The ones that did, she didn't want to move in with. Ultimately, she moved her things down to Mark's, with whom she was just friends, and lived companionably with him as a housemate. She made a number of trips with her big frame pack carrying a few more things each time. Finally her plastic house was empty. He stood inside its empty shell and watched the rain fall down from the trees and run in little runnels down the inside of the poles. She had moved away.

Ryan visited her at Mark's. He sat with the two of them by the big wood stove in the kitchen of the old log house. Sometimes he had dinner with them, and slept with her occasionally in the little log bedroom where her arrowheads and pictures from the past were now arrayed. She was helping Mark with the canning and storing of root crops. She helped him gather maple leaves to cover the garden. She told Ryan that Mark and she were not lovers, just friends and roommates. Ryan asked her if now maybe they could get back together as just an ordinary couple. She said she did not know. She wanted him to do something, make something of his life, not to be so aimless, unfocused and living from day to day. He told her that he believed he had come into the world to do something important, to accomplish some task, but that he didn't know what it was yet. He said that he believed that in some way he was preparing for it now, turning the blank brown soil so that the seed could fall from heaven. She simply said, "That's really far out," but it didn't change her mind.

In late Autumn, when the wheel of the year was moving toward a complete turn since their first meeting, Selene told him that she was leaving, going back to Oregon for a few months to hang out with old friends and straighten out her head. The night before she left she invited him over to Mark's to spend the night with her. She said that Mark was in Vancouver so they would have the homestead to themselves. They cooked dinner, drank a bit of wine and talked late into the night. They went to bed to make love, both of them feeling it was for the last time. It was tender and caring. They licked away each other's tears. She left a candle burning all night and they held each other and sighed as the wind ruffled the plastic windows and the flame flickered. In the middle of the night, when he stepped out of the house to pee, early snowflakes were beginning to swirl down through the trees. Some stuck in his hair. "It's snowing," he whispered when he climbed back into bed. He held her and told her that he wished there was something he could do to get her to change her mind.

He said, "I've never known anyone quite like you and never loved anyone in quite the same way."

She simply said, "I know."

They got up early, lit the fire, and made some coffee and breakfast. Inside, they could only see the blurry white light that came through the plastic windows, so they stood in the doorway, coffee cups in hand, arms around each other and watched the world slowly being dusted white. They pretended that the homestead was a glass ball that had been shaken to make the snowflakes fall, a tiny circumscribed world where it could just be she and he. They watched the white begin to fill in between the clumps of swamp grass that tufted the ancient field, watched it coat the remaining maple leaves. They waited like this until they heard the truck that was coming up the dirt road to pick her up—the outside world coming into their crystal dome. He helped her carry her pack, her bundle of arrowheads, her case of jars and herbs, her box of books and photos out to the truck. She climbed into the cab with the driver, waved, and then they drove away. He went back into the house.

He just sat in Mark's rocking chair and rolled a cigarette and smoked it while the snow fell around the house. He reflected on how they had gotten together on the last snow of the previous year and now, on the first snow of this year, she had left—a relationship that had lasted from snow to snow.

He listened to the sound of the truck recede in the distance. When it was gone he listened to the remains of the morning fire popping in the stove. His lungs were raw and sore from smoking and he decided that, at this juncture of change, he would give up smoking; he decided that he had the power to do that. He decided that this would be his last cigarette.

He sat and rocked by the warm wood stove and savoured the last few puffs. It would take an enormous summoning of will to carry this through and before finishing the cigarette he realised that he must give up Selene too, his attachment to her, his love for her, his sexual slavery to her; that he must simply put her out of

114

his mind; not think of her anymore; that when he found himself thinking of her, he must move his mind elsewhere; re-create his life without her.

He finished the cigarette and threw the butt into the wood stove. There were only a few dying embers left. He did the breakfast dishes and left them in the rack so that Mark would not come back to a dirty kitchen. He damped down the stove, put on his hat and coat, and closed the door, leaving Mark's empty house behind him. He walked home through the snow, feeling the white emptiness of it, allowing its coolness and peace to enter him.

X
Trails

Winter walks about.

The night prowls on winds through the dark landscape.

There are friendly little trails that I travel under the second growth trees to the old houses where my friends live.

Hello, I am Ryan, his ghost. I get tired of that old man who I turned into writing about me. He uses my voice as though it's me talking, but he is all thought and no action. I'd like to talk for myself awhile, talk about how it feels in my time rather than from his far retrospect.

I do wonder how I got myself into this, living in this hobbity world full of tiny wood heated houses connected by a network of trails. Oh yes, there are also roads, but they are kept open by the orange road grader and orange road truck, driven by the men in orange hard hats. Later, I get to know these men and their families; they are Sven and Thom, really just ordinary men but it feels like they are from another time, left over dinosaurs, which is really disturbing since, reflecting on it, I realise that they are just the representatives of the going culture, its ambassadors, in this strange place.

Really, we are the strange ones, not them. We live a retro lifestyle—using wood technology and hand tools scrounged from used shops in dirty city cores—and think of this as salvaging what is salvageable from our civilisation—believing that we are somehow its future. We use trails instead of public roadways, living in a hidden world that is only partly visible from the road.

It's true that if you are Thom sitting in his road grader eating your lunch you can see our houses. You can see the smoke that comes out of the chimney and the person—the long haired man in work clothes or the woman in a flowing shift—that comes out of the door to say hello and talk about the weather and the garden, but, really, who are these people? As the graderman you have lived through the depression and are glad for the security of your government job. You can see that some of us are poor, but certainly not all of us: some are educated, having dropped out from teaching or other professions. You know that we could be doing much better for ourselves than this. You must wonder what makes us tick.

You know that there must be drugs involved: you have seen our strange behaviour at the dances at the Legion. You reluctantly invited us because the small numbers on the island made any guests better than continuing on with the same fifteen people who had been drinking, waltzing, playing bingo with each other for as long as you can remember. You have seen the strange things we do there, like when James took off his clothes and danced in naked ecstasy. As the graderman you were probably both appalled and fascinated. You realise that The Rules are gone, or much attenuated. Once The Rules are gone what is there to protect you from yourself, your desires, the dark side of rage and murder, your lust for other men's wives? Shit, you can't just go around fucking everybody!

You fear that the veneer of civilisation is being ripped off by these people living in the abandoned homesteads in this isolated place. The island is so alone and secluded after the last ferry of the day has left, so separate from the consensual world of shopping malls and gas stations with clean restrooms. On Wednesday and Thursday there is no ferry at all. You are all alone with the shushing of the winds and your own strange self. What would happen without The Rules? The island is a world of its own with its own society and its own laws; you know that it can spread, spread to you, your wife, your sons.

In fact, Thom's son Harry did have his brains blown out in one of the old cabins that had housed a succession of single men and woman who were refugees from relationship chaos. There had been a drunken fight at the Legion and someone followed him home and blew his brains out. The house was abandoned after that, the door left open to blow in the wind. The kids went there after school to see the artefacts of violent death. For months afterwards they talked about the stains on the wall behind the bed where Harry had fought his last battle.

At the time of his demise Harry was wearing my father's leather air force jacket. He had borrowed it from me on a cold winter night and had refused to return it, even though I had asked him so many times. Rumour had it that he went home and passed out fully dressed on the bed. The person he had fought with had gone home, got a gun and come into his house. He woke him up and they struggled and swore at each other a bit and then the gun was fired. I never had the guts to ask his parents about the jacket after he had got his brains blown out in it.

My father also drank himself to death—the end is always from something else though. For my father it was cancer; for Harry it was getting his brains blown out. I always wondered about Harry's affinity for that jacket. It almost makes me believe in Vibes or in Karma, makes me believe that in taking the jacket, he somehow took my father's mantle from my shoulders and carried it for me; that somehow, with his own life, he extinguished that legacy so that I didn't have to live it out.

But, you see, that is the way I think, a kind of symbolic, magical thinking, blended with the concepts of many religions: my own hodgepodge of wisdom and superstition. It's a problem that comes from looking at life as though it is literature. That's what I mean about the grader and the houses. You can park outside with the motor idling and eat your lunch; you can say a few kind words to the person who comes out to say hello; you can even benevolently accept that person, as Thom, kindly by nature, did; but you still wonder what their life behind the social façade is really like. And unless you create that special relationship where you become an easy familiar and are allowed into their household, you will never know.

It is the same with knowing a person: who is it behind those eyes, behind the pleasantries, the witty exchanges, or the stolid dullness. What is this well we

120

call a human being? If we travel downward—or upward—through all its layers, diving in, what do we find, and is it the same or different than ourselves? So, since the main roads rarely take you beyond the façade, this chapter, my chapter, is about trails, entry routes.

The roads on the island were born out of industry, the need to take out the logs and float them away. They followed the contours of the ledges and valleys that were level enough for the big trucks to travel over. Often they ended at log dumps, which today are decaying platforms of whole tree trunks projecting out over the waters of some little bay that now sleeps quietly in its mud, sand and clams. Once, so long ago, they bustled with winches, choker cables, steam donkeys; men shouting and signing over the noise of their machines.

Ecological disaster has come and gone. The island has already been subjected to predation, stripped of everything it had to offer except solitude, and been left for years to quietly heal itself. It has been left alone as worthless. Not even the real estate tycoons and subdividers have cottoned on to it yet. It is a good place for us to heal ourselves, but, most of the time, we don't even know that is what we are doing: we are just living, trying to find some sort of life in the midst of the suffering and political chaos around us. We are just

*learning to cut firewood, grow vegetables and take care
of goats and chickens.*

*Maria Montessori says that children in their
developmental stages must play with primitive shelter
and cook food on open fires. John Holt, another figure
of my time, says that children recapitulate evolution in
the womb and then human history in early childhood.
He says, for instance, that six year old boys are proud,
competitive and loyal, like classical Greeks. So perhaps
this is all we are doing, making up for a skipped
developmental phase, reconnecting with the earth and
the rhythm of the seasons. Perhaps it's a developmental
phase that our whole civilisation, as it spins out of
control, has missed. We eat mushrooms, drink home
brew, plant gardens and rediscover nature worship. Was
it reading the hobbit that did this to us? Or perhaps it is
doomsday sunk deep in our souls: the mushroom shaped
death head of Hiroshima, rising again and again on our
TV screens. The ancient lie of Armageddon. Yes,
perhaps we are just trying to start over in the face of a
civilisation, a world, that seems about to be swept away
like a magician's table cloth. In my more optimistic
moods, I get Buddhist about the whole thing and think
the bomb is just the Horn of the Dharma, banishing the
ego by presenting it with death. Death is everywhere, if*

not outside—nuclear war, earthquakes, car accidents—then inside—cancer and other failings of the body.

The old logging roads go a long way around to avoid passing over private property. For instance, to get from my corner to the Valley House you have to go a mile down Main road to the lake. The lake was once a small lake, but was hastily dammed and filled to provide water for the community of False Bay. Around its margin, dead firs still stand like ghosts of the former forest, their silver skeletons poking up through the dark waters. During winter freezes, you can walk in this dead forest, venture out on skates, the ice cracking and groaning under your feet, making noises that sound like messages from outer space. You can actually stand under these drowned trees and touch them, before returning cautiously to the road and to safety. Also near this lake, back in the alders under the rising bluffs, is the remainder of a cabin. Only a few rotten poles are left and you really have to know where to look. Rumour has it that thirty years ago a woman lived there alone. That is all that is known. Another haunting.

At the lake you turn left on another dirt road and then travel back a mile almost the way you came, on a winding, twisted road through wrecked logging land. You wind up at the Valley House, only a quarter mile away from where you started, as the crow flies, but two miles away by road.

The Valley House, true to its name is a small one-story house that sits on the edge of a long valley full of empty fields turning back into Labrador tea swamps. The first time I saw it, I had been walking on the harsh logging road, surfaced with large chunks of sharp broken rock. I came over the bluff and there it sat, down below me, yellow, empty and spooky. For some reason it still had its glass windows.

It had a strange feeling even then. If it had been a movie, scary music would have played when it came into view. It just looked like a haunted house. The people who came to live there a year later, refugees from Los Angeles, said that there was a rocking chair they could hear going all night long. A mother with a dry cough sat in it and tried to hush her baby to sleep. There was also a phantom truck that would pull up in the middle of the night, shut off its headlights and turn off the motor. My friends would wait to see who it was and when nobody got out, they would go out the front door with flashlights to see who was there. No one was there, no truck, no nothing! Da da da da, da da da da. It happened again and again.

Right in front of the Valley House, the road splits in two. One branch continues down the valley to the

124

water where the moon sets. The other goes back around the head of the valley and then continues down to the water on the valley's other side. The creek from this shallow swampy valley ends up at a little bay where there is yet another deserted cabin.

All the cabins were empty back then. Little did I know that soon, within several years, all these broken down houses would be lived in by refugees drawn, like myself, to the island's isolation. They began to fill, one by one, with people who stapled plastic over the empty window frames, found an old wood stove in a junkyard and moved right in. I found myself again in a society, a community, as others began to create lives of human interaction here, bringing with them what they could not leave behind.

While this was happening, I had started to live in a smaller and smaller world. First I gave up having a car and walked almost everywhere or got rides. As a result I started living closer and closer to home, spending most of my time with neighbours who lived within half an hour's walk. Even visiting friends at the south end of the island became a long journey, usually necessitating spending the night. Thus these visits were only carried out once or twice a year, on rare occasions.

I spent a lot of time exploring the area right around my house. Not exactly infinity in the palm of your hand, but something like that. Each day in spring I would walk up to the meadows behind Smedley's to look for morels or pick wild daffodils. In fall I would search the little second growth forest there for chanterelles. On a little side trail I found an old dump and spent some time digging up antique bottles.

Also in spring, the Amanita Muscaria fruited and their brown buttons with white specks poked up everywhere. There was a popular book that claimed that the real meaning of the Sacrament—what eating the flesh of Jesus really referred to—was not some wimpy little wafer of Wonder Bread, but the eating of Amanita Muscaria. Of course, since the mushroom came up everywhere, we just had to give it a try. Some Amanitas are very poisonous so we started with little tiny chunks, several days apart, and began increasing the dose until we started to feel something.

Once people on the island got their personal dose right, the woods began to look like some kind of faery land during Amanita season. On a nice day people wandered through the forest, shafts of light coming down like saintly sunbeams, munching as they went. I ran into the Valley House people more than once. We all wore toques in early spring so everybody looked like those plaster lawn dwarves with coloured hats: Sleepy, Dopey, Grumpy and so on. To get high on Amanita

Muscaria you had to take enough so that it affected your motor co-ordination, so everybody was stumbling around, or sitting, or just standing like a lawn ornament.

If you took too much, then your body wouldn't work and you'd just have to lie down and enter the psychic realm into which the mushroom took you. It would have its way with you. Selene and I had taken some once when it became clear that things weren't working out between us. We were trying to find a metaphysical realm in which all things, including our strange relationship, seemed possible. After eating "the flesh of the gods" we lay down on the bed together, a bit of sunlight coming through the window. We just lay in each other's arms, parking our bodies into each other's keeping, and travelled out together. It was interesting because we shared many parts of our out of body adventure. We were so close then. It was as though our bodies being entwined somehow kept our spirits together in the realm into which we entered.

She flew before me and after me. I ascended great columns of air and clouds while she fell or floated down on the other side. At one point we entered a huge machine. We were surrounded by skyscraper high towers of electrical wirings, wound armatures, that propelled us with their fields up and down. We'd touch bottom and be propelled upward to the top and sink

127

down again like we were on a huge electronically amplified trampoline. Then we got out of sync and she was going up while I was going down. I'd just catch a glimpse of her in passing and then I'd watch her disappear into a tiny speck before we started coming back toward each other. She seemed to be enjoying it but I wanted to get back in sync with her. Being out of sync was too much like what was happening to us in the rest of our life. I felt that if I could catch her here, in the inner world, harmony would come in the outer world as well, but it was not meant to be. I did a bunch of calculations and realized that if I pushed off the bottom at just the right moment I would come into sync. I tried it and my whole body jerked and it woke both of us up. Selene was cross. She looked at me with bewildered eyes and said "Why did you wake me?" Then she dropped back into her visions.

Toward the end of our relationship, Selene moved out of my house into a small plastic house that she had built in the forest, mostly to explore relationships with other men. I had loved her deeply in a relationship that had lasted from the last snowfall of one year to the first of the next. It was one of those disastrous and boundaryless relationship experiments that were so characteristic of my time. We rejected the feelings of

128

jealousy and pain as something that must be moved beyond, as the product of old tapes and bad conditioning. Was this the legacy of Marxism filtering down to us? Rarely did we go to the source of ideas then or wonder where they came from. We simply floated around in the zeitgeist, living second hand ideas that had somehow gripped the culture and taken on power. One of these was alternative forms of sexual/marital arrangements.

It never occurred to us that feelings of jealousy were hardwired and had to be honoured and talked about—the nature of the beast. We were trying to transcend them, trying to transcend our own natures, and it did not occur to us that we were, in actuality, violating our own natures. I learned about the animal during one of those times when Selene was not with me, I went to a party and found Selene there with one of her men. They had their arms around each other. The party was in one of those old log houses with plastic stapled over the empty window frames. Gusts of rain were spattering against the plastic which was flapping in the storm. People were drinking and laughing and playing music by the light of smoking kerosene lamps. The candles wavered every time a gust of wind came through the permeable house. With no electricity, we had returned to making our own music, for better or worse, trying to find some importance in our own little lives, which, until now, had been overshadowed by the lives and music of the greatly talented who dominated the mass culture.

I stood at the back of the dark room and was amazed at the tightness in my chest, the hair standing up on the back of my neck, the adrenaline and rage that were flowing in my body. I left and walked the anguish off in miles on the dark dirt roads, going to visit Isaac in the middle of the night. This was a force to be reckoned with, this primitive reaction. It was not easily wished away, or wished away at all. The animal spirit that carried me around had its thousands of years of instinct, its recipe for survival. It had its reasons. It howled at the moon and was embedded deeply into my flesh. Stags charge each other out in the autumn meadows. Perhaps loggers in the pub at Youbou are being more honest when they bray and bash each other's heads in over minor infractions.

There were a few exceptions, but, in general, people were living the spring-time of relationship over and over, the hot passionate part. When it cooled down, we moved to another, new hot passionate relationship. We didn't want to be like our parents, living relationships of desiccated bickering and the embittered execution of chores. When sexual passion faded we took it as a sign that something was wrong, that the magic had left. And then we looked for more magic. When my friend Lorenzo visited his parents after breaking up with his latest girl friend, who they had liked, they asked him why. He said, simply, "Because we stopped loving each other." His parents snarled back at him "What the hell does love have to do with a god-damned marriage?"

Selene had a fantasy of a great floating, wooden-hulled dome that followed the unfolding of spring up and down the pacific coast. As the northern summer waned, this craft followed the sun south into the tropics. After it crossed the equator, it would float into the southern temperate zone just in time to catch early spring, the buds just beginning to open. It followed the blossoms south for as long as it could, until, at its most southern point, the summer began to turn to autumn. Then it would turn north again toward the tropics, keeping just ahead of winter. On the northern side of the equator it would catch the beginning of the northern spring and follow it northward, prolonging its time in the blossoming for as long as it could. This magical craft had flowers and fields under its dome, all tended by beautiful young men and women in the spring of their life, all deeply in love with each other and freed from the afflictions of possessiveness and jealousy.

Many years later I was listening to the CBC and heard a Jungian analyst ask why Zeus, the most promiscuous of gods—swans, bulls, golden rain, anything to get laid—was married to insanely jealous Hera, protector of the sanctity of the family. Was it a mismatch? The analyst felt it was just a mythic externalisation of two parts of us: when we get too far into Zeus, Hera comes up and puts an end to it, starts lopping off heads and laying down curses. Hera was coming up big time in me.

Earlier, in a time of loneliness and desolation, I had taken some acid. In the initial stages of the trip, I had washed the dishes and swept the floor as usual. I can see why yogis bathe and sweep every day. Selene had said that coming on to Acid is like dying, letting go of our current life and coming back into a life that is changed by the insight and experience of the drug. It is a death and a rebirth, and I certainly didn't want to come back to an old mess. On this particular day, the experience was too overwhelming. I was too full of feeling and needed help. I needed to be held. I could not stand, for one more time, the dissolution of my psyche.

Selene was at the Valley House having a brief affair with Andy. It was humiliating to go, to be in such need, to not be the master of my own ship, but I went, following the familiar trail.

The drug was thrumming through my veins, and the universe was leaking in from everywhere, obliterating my frail form. I felt like I was trying to reach her before my dissolution. Somewhere near half way, I could show you the exact spot, it became too much. I felt I was dying, that I was spreading out into the universe. Death, the last frontier.

I sat down in the September grass and my consciousness expanded through infinite space. I was terrified. It felt like if I stayed there any longer I would leave my body and die. I only wish I had known about Grof's work then; had found some sort of compassionate guide to talk me through these explorations.

Somehow I forced myself back down into my body and continued down the trail, shot through with light, a conglomeration of light, thoughts, and cells, wearing a Mexican shirt, hair tied with a head band. I was in fear. In my chest was the grief of losing Selene, the grief that I had been ignoring with booze and drugs, but now on acid, another drug, this loss was being magnified.

As I got to the lower cow swamp, I heard drums coming from the Valley House. I wondered, "Can you go to a house and drag a woman who you have been close to—who you are still close to—away from her new *man and ask for help, for love, for healing?" There was no-one else to turn to. I felt shame at having to do it but there was no choice, the imperative of terror and grief was so big that I felt like I was about to explode. Selene had been my healer as well as my lover over the last year. From her grandmother she had learned to move pain out of the body and down an arm or leg and out the toes or fingers. Many times she had done this for me, and my body had become lighter and less burdened. Afterwards she wiped her hands on a small clean towel that she always brought to the session.*

I realized that I must go to the door and knock; that I must contain myself and ask whoever came to the door if I could speak to Selene. In the future I came to realise that an aspect of relationship that had been overlooked in my time was the aspect of needing help, of having someone on your side, of having someone to tell your deepest fears and to hold you in the night. Relationship seemed to be viewed in terms of passion and celebration, and when the party was over it was time to move on. Fritz Pearls wrote "I do my thing, you do yours, if we meet fine, if not it can't be helped." Perhaps useful as a formula for coming out of cold, dead, relationships, but what a terrible self-sufficiency it presupposed. I was just trying to stay in human form, not be totally dissolved. I needed help.

The perennial party of the L.A crazies was going on: the drums, the homebrew, somebody playing the flute. Even standing at the bend in the road, looking through the trunks and foliage of the young alders, I could smell the intoxicating smell of hashish floating in the late summer air, along with the smell of the distant sea, along with the smell of rotting leaves from the swamp, the somniferous smell of the Labrador tea plants, the smell of wild mint, the smell of the cow and sheep dung that littered the fields. The smell was of life/death, growth/decay, which is really what this event we live should be called: "How's your life/death, growth/decay going today?"

These memories are the richly embroidered ghosts that follow me everywhere, that attach themselves to the places and people of my life. There are also the other ghosts of what could be and what could have been, the hope and regret that spring eternal. Some people say that these are the cause of our suffering and that the cure is to be in the Here and Now, but all these are happening in the Here and Now. They are the flitting illusions that follow and lead us like our own depraved Greek chorus, directing the comedy or tragedy of our lives. Might as well just hit ourselves over the head with a sledge hammer if we don't want them.

So, there I was, trying to get up my courage to go and knock on the door. That is just another memory now, but then it was hot and painful. I heard the laughter, the joking, the music coming from the house and was afraid that if I went to the door I would be laughed at or joked about. I gathered myself as best I could to act normal. I knew that I would be invited in and I didn't want to go in. I just couldn't do that, say hello to everybody, pretend everything was OK, so I just knocked, hoping that it would be Dorrie who got the door, but it was Ron, a friend from LA who seemed a little quieter, a little more introspective than the rest. He took me in for a moment with his dark Semitic eyes. I said, in my most normal voice, "Hi Ron, is Selene here?"

He smiled at me, "Sure man, how are you, come on in."

"I'm kind of freaking out," I said, "There's just too many people in there; would you mind asking her if she would come out for a minute?"

Ron smiled; I could see that this was all right with him, that it seemed like a reasonable request. He had seen a lot worse than this. He said "sure man," again, and walked back into the dark house, leaving the door open, leaving me standing on the porch in the late morning sun. A moment later Selene was standing in

136

front of me. She was wearing the jeans that she almost always wore and a light green, faded T-shirt. Around her neck she wore the small arrowhead that she had found out on the lava flows of northern California where the Modoc had made their last stand.

Her face wrinkled into a smile when she saw me, "Wow, you look really stoned," she said.

"Yeah," I said, "I dropped Acid and I'm freaking out, it's more pain than I can stand, I think I am dying, my body keeps dissolving. I'm scared. Can you spend a little time with me? I'm really frightened."

She is one of the few people who knows how afraid of dying I am, how I worry about cancer eating me away like it did my father. It's funny the things we know about people when we really get close to them. It's terrible to lose somebody who is that close, to be stranded out on the beaches of conventional conversation again while the tide is coming in all around.

She laughed and took my hand and pulled me to her in a brief hug. "Yes, I'll be right out." She went back into the house while I waited. What did she say to the people inside? What did she say to Andy, or did she say anything at all? She grabbed her buckskin coat with the fringes on it and came out the door. "I only have a little time," she said in a kindly way, "where shall we go?"

"Let's walk," I said. She took my hand and we walked as far as the bend in the road, just out of sight of the house. I was beginning to dissolve again and huge sobs were starting to rise from within me. I was feeling the loss of her warmth, of her love for me, of the treasure of having her as a travelling companion on this slippery highway, of her Tarot cards, of her charts, of the stacks of blue ephemerides that used to stand on the shelf in my house, of her Indian artifacts that used to line my window sills. I felt like a ship that had lost its navigator. On one hand she was a priestess that could chart the way. On the other she was just a girl who liked drugs and variety in her sex, or maybe she was a bacchante, a priestess who surrendered to the urges of the goddess and let them transform her. It depended on how you looked at it.

"Can we sit?" I asked?"

"Where?" she said.

I looked around. We were at a place where there was nowhere to sit. The road was surrounded by a thicket of tiny alders about half the size of my arm. There was no rock, no bluff to look out from, no stream to sit beside.

"How 'bout just in the trees?" I said.

"OK," she said, and we pushed through the spindly stems until we found an opening big enough to

138

sit in. She took off her buckskin coat and laid it down on last year's crackly leaves. We sat in the late summer as motionless as a couple of deer hiding in a thicket. "I'm so frightened," I said, "Can you hold me?" And she said "sure," her eyes and voice full of kindness. I leaned into her and she took me in her arms while I sobbed and wept and shook.

When the fury passed, I sat up and we talked. We were trying to help each other. We were no longer lovers, that had ended badly, but we were friends. No one seemed to have wives, or steady girl friends, or anyone consistent to turn to, not since The Disintegration had hit. We intended to expand our consciousness, that's what we called it, but feeling all this loss, this great load of grief that each of us carried from the loss of our culture, our parents, our wives and husbands, our children, the lovers who we'd left behind, was so painful. Our inevitable deaths lay before us, and beyond that, the great sparkling universe. We were all blown apart by this, living on the edge of a shimmering void into which all things threatened to be sucked. Here we camped, doing our best to create our little human lives.

We were like participants in a children's crusade, trying to help each other with poorly understood bits of ancient wisdom that seemed to describe some of what we were experiencing. Without any guides we went forward only to be mowed down by the genies we had released. You'd think we would have stopped taking the little pills that said "EAT ME," but it seemed, at the time, that we had opened a Pandora's box and that the only way out was all the way through to the other side. We submitted, time after time, to this cleansing.

And sometimes, on the other side of loss and rampantly marching death, there was a sparkling clarity in which we knew ourselves as bigger than this human form. And we knew that the beauty of the planet, with its twisted trees, its bare rock bluffs, its shimmering seas, its great storms, its blue skies, its family of creatures that hovered and crawled was really who we were. For some moments we were lifted beyond our personal melodrama and glimpsed a picture that was so grand and magnificent—billions of stars being born, blazing and sputtering out in the sky—that we committed again and again to this process. We needed to be willing to expand beyond our little shells, to stand with our raw flesh open to the universe, if we wished to witness this grand stage before the final exeunt all.

We were like midwives to each other, like medieval mendicants on pilgrimage. We lived hidden lives, far from those who would never understand. I dried my eyes, having somewhat discharged my great cloud of sorrow. I looked at Selene. Even though she was with another man now, I saw the love and caring in her eyes. She gently stroked my hand.

"It's a long journey," she said, "and we must find faith along the way, trust that it all works out. We can't just stop and cling to each other out of fear. We must go on." And in this moment I believed her. She talked about many things that I could only understand at a deep intuitive level in my altered state; not something I can explain or understand today.

The sounds of the party entered my awareness again, the muffled thrumming of the guitar, the beat of the drum, the sound of voices raised in song. I realised that I was keeping her from her new life, the change that was taking her away from me. It was time for her to go. I felt immensely grateful that she had helped and comforted me.

Out on the road we said good bye and I watched her walk back to the Valley House with that unintentionally sexy walk she had. She looked over her shoulder and smiled as she disappeared around the bend. I turned back to the road and then to the trail. It was now a tapestry of tiny white daisies that were growing up through the grass. I had, for the moment released the heaviness inside and forgiven myself for my transgressions. For the moment I was not worried about

141

where it was all going. For the moment I had let go of my distant wife and daughter. For the moment, life seemed sufficient just as it was.

I walked on this trail feeling the dry grass of late summer under my bare feet. My head felt like it was in the clouds and the sun was shining in on me. So I went home, stretched between heaven and earth, partaking of both. Just for the moment I could let go of my sad little tale. Just for the moment.

XI
The Mountain

The mountain rises 1130 feet above the sea. It does not stand alone like a miniature Mount Fuji, but is one of many bluffs—the highest of them—that rise up out of the island's undulating forest. From impossible cracks, ancient bonsais twisted by the wind, grow in its bare basalt cliffs. From the top, you can look down on everything: lakes, fields, forest, everything laid out at your feet. The surrounding islands are set into the watery curve of the earth. You can look down the great gulch of water that separates Vancouver Island from the mainland and see the mountains on either side, two rows of white peaks through which the ceaseless tides flow.

As the highest and steepest mountain on the island, it has resisted the forest the longest. Many of the island's other peaks have succumbed completely, given up their long views to sleep peacefully under the spreading boughs of firs. Only a few, like this one, have remained bare rock and still look fiercely out over the land and sea below.

Listen! In the beginning there was nothing but bare rock, thrust up out of the water. Lichen—half fungus, half algae—began to eat it away. Over the centuries it got thick enough for grass seed, brought in by wind and bird, to grow. The new grass dropped its seed and generations of grass, rising, falling, dying, gave rise to enough soil for the first little pines to grow.

The pines went to seed early and died of summer drought; their roots found only rock; their dead bodies blew down, cracked by whipping winds. Over the centuries they decayed, slowly because of the dryness, but eventually turned into soil that could hold just a little more water. The next generation of pines grew just a little larger and then they too fell. On most of the bluffs, generation after generation of these dwarf forests rose and fell, each a little bigger than the one before. Slowly, with the help of insects and fungus, the soil grew, finally becoming a damp sponge that held enough water for the first fir seeds to sprout and live.

All this while, the firs had been stalking up the bluffs, preceded by an army of alders that grew and died in front of them like foot soldiers, laying down their bodies to become soil. Finally the firs reached the top. They started to engulf the bluffs; dropped their needles, century after century, until the forest floor was thick with salal and sword fern. A climax forest it is called.

The mountain was a stage on which this panorama of life rising out of death played itself out. It was also the stage on which Ryan usually had his experiences with psychedelics. Seeing all this with time lapse-eyes, he also saw that humanity was such a forest, growing, sacrificing, striving, falling—generation after generation—toward some obscure climax expression of itself. He thought that one way to achieve happiness might be to sense and serve this greater destiny.

During his time, the mountain top was mostly bare rock. At its northern edge was just a small grove of pines growing out of the twisted broken bodies of the pine generations that had come and gone before. Straight rock faces plunged hundreds of feet down; several winding trails replete with hand holds went to the top. There was a jar with pencils and paper where people left notes and poems.

Ryan's first adventure on acid opened a new world for him. It became for him like space to the astronaut, sky for a pilot, the deeps to a diver, the sea for a sailor, the peaks to a mountaineer. Like them, he did not take these sallies lightly. He equipped himself for each trip

145

and only made the journey at long intervals. Yet, the mysterious heights invariably drew him back again. In all, he had ascended maybe a dozen times, over several years, but it changed him, changed the way he looked at himself; at the world; at life.

Ever since he could remember, he had looked for the newness of life. As a child he had gone forward to each new amazement. As he grew up, the circle of familiarity grew bigger and he became knowledgeable, masterful, an expert, but also trapped in the circle's ordinariness. In university he had explored the microscopic and the macroscopic, strange cultures, foreign cities, but nothing held his interest for long. It all seemed like more of the same. Selene had told him that it was a west coast thing: that the people who moved west were the ones who were dissatisfied with their little homesteads; once the last picket was nailed on the fence, the farm didn't hold their interest anymore; they caught the next wagon train west, farm after farm, until there was nowhere left to go. Then, there they stood looking out across the Pacific, where strange ideas from Asia came floating up onto the shore like glass fishing balls or messages in bottles. She said that all this moving imposed a process of natural selection: those who arrived on the coast were the restless seekers who loved the exploring more than the settling. There was nowhere left to go but inward, the inner frontier. Their descendents, and there were many of us, carried their restless genes. That was Selene's theory.

Ryan had learned that there are gates and guardians that one must pass through to arrive at the realm of free energies. There was death, or at least a ritual death, to go through, but it seemed real enough at the time, as though his body could just dissolve, as though the bonds that held all those rotating electrons in place around those balls of protons and neutrons that he remembered from school could just fly apart—poof—fire dissolving into air.

In the early stages of coming on to the drug he tuned into his body, or rather, his bodily sensations were gradually amplified until he could no longer ignore them. He came to feel every bit of the pain that he carried around with him, that he had learned to block out, preferring most of the time to live in a world that was relatively dead and dull rather than endure so much sensation and feeling.

Gurdieff taught that enlightenment was the product of hard work, the product of using herculean tasks to push the ego beyond its capacities until it broke down and revealed the greater consciousness in which it was housed. A student once asked Gurdieff, put off by his Russian, suffering approach to enlightenment, "What if science invented a pill that enlightened people. What would you do?" Without hesitation Gurdieff—we see his mustachios, his one drooping eye, his bald circus strong man's skull—answered "Take pill, of course."

In Victoria, Ryan had seen a great domed church. It was at the top of a hill looking down through a leafy boulevard over the lower city. Cars streamed past it. It looked as though it was once magnificent but was now out of place, forgotten, in the encroachment of streets and thoroughfares. It had a rounded portico supported by columns. On the lintel was inscribed "First Church of Christ, Scientist." For him it brought to mind the image of a Protestant Christ with neatly combed long hair and a short trimmed beard. He looked something like a hip UBC academic in a clean white lab coat. He was in a modern laboratory, surrounded by Bunsen burners and retorts. In his hand was a test tube that he was holding up to the light. Having over the centuries taught prayer, devotion, fasting, all to little avail; having even undergone crucifixion in a generous but ineffective attempt to save this stubborn race, he was now resorting to chemistry, cooking up a pill that would bring people in droves to his beloved father. One suspected, however, that he might have kept this little science experiment to himself; that perhaps he had not told his beloved father; that perhaps this selfsame loving father may not have entirely given his blessing to his son's new project. The doors to heaven and hell. Some went straight to heaven while others saw hell. To J.C. it seemed like a winner either way. Some found their way to heaven; others had the B-Jesus scared out of them and spent the rest of their lives seeking refuge in faith. Many a fundamentalist has arrived there through the ministration of drugs.

Once, in the early days of taking acid, the pain had driven Ryan out of his house into a thicket of broom that grew across the road. He hid there like a wounded deer. The pain and achiness were so intense that he felt like ripping off his skin and muscles; he fell to the ground, suppressing the groans that wanted to come from his lips. After that had passed, he sat up and wove the broom plants around him into a green dome, tying them at the top with their own branches. He made a little hut like his father used to build for him as a child. He sat in it, sheltered from the passing world, listening to the odd truck pass along main road. Later a couple walked by, laughing about a dinner party that had gone wrong. When he crawled out of the hut and stood on the road again, he was temporarily freed of the cumulative tensions that he usually wore like a suit of armour: the tensions of growing up, of acting right at school, acting right at home, of competition, of exams (even then, he still dreamt of his pencil continually breaking while his paper remained empty), of restraining his sexuality, of broken relationships, of the concealed parts of himself that he never let anyone see, of mustering the courage to express other parts of himself, of feeling excluded by those around him, of competing for inclusion and affection, of a creature knowing that he would die, of the death of his father, of his loneliness for his far-away daughter, of the bomb hanging over all their heads. It was a time when John Lennon was screaming his primal pain over the radio: "Momma don't go, Daddy stay hoooooooome." Of all this he was momentarily relieved.

Having, like a drowning man, just seen his life pass before his eyes, he left his hut, his kiva, a 23 year old boy-man, his long frizzy hair tied with a reed circlet, temporarily bathed of all that, and walked back into a world unfiltered by his conditioning and sparkling in all its beauty. He had passed through the gravitational field of his personal pain into the weightlessness of living for a short while as a spirit on the earth. Gone, Gone Beyond, Gone Way Beyond, Gone Beyond-The-Beyond, Gone Way Beyond Beyond-The-Beyond, Way Gone Way Way Beyond Beyond-The-Beyond. So be it.

He did wonder after each dissolution why he did not stop. Many did: they took a few trips, enjoyed heaven until, ambushed by death, by hell, by inner and outer demons they dropped back to the pleasures of beer and a little pot; tried to forget the vast and scary world that had once opened up before them. As his spiritual insight faded into memory, he came to feel numb again: just another person pointlessly weeding a garden, repairing fences, living out a meaningless broken life. Seeking some insight that was medicine for this, he would one day clean his house again, shower in his little shower that was heated by coils around the chimney pipe, put on clean clothes and take the drug. It was usually on a day when the ferry didn't run and the island was quiet. He would enter this world only occasionally at the pain of the truly frightening death experience. He was called upon to summon the requisite bravery. He dropped the tiny pill at home and then traveled, by road and trail, high onto the shoulder of the mountain. There the trail ended and he scuffled up the rest of the way along the forest floor, through thickets of salal and arrow wood, to the mountain's top.

I've waited too long, I think, tidying up around the house. I went out the door with my pack on but then I saw all the wood chips littering the front yard and got the rake and cleaned them up, and then I saw a broken board on the porch and just had to pull it off and cut another one to fix it. One thing led to another until the acid was thrumming in my body and the world was becoming alive with movement and I had needed to put my tools away and close the gate behind me. Actually, I didn't really put the tools away but arranged them neatly on the chopping block where I would see them when I came home. They looked beautiful there, like a collage, but I could already see the rust moving through the steel, beginning the slow process of dissolution that would take place over the centuries, so I decided I'd better leave, NOW!

I wanted to be up in the forest when it came on, but it is too late for that now. I just hadn't wanted to be confronted by a mess when I returned home. So now I am on main road walking quickly to get to the trail to Mark's, anxious to be in the shelter of the trees, alone, private. I already feel the well of emotion about the loss of Selene, the sadness and fear, which has been bringing me down lately. It is rising to the surface, a cumulative pain of all this and of all humanity aching in my body. The last place I want to be with all this happening is on Main Road. With my pack and water bottle I must look like just another hiker walking jauntily along.

I can hear a truck coming from far away, from the South End. I hear it a long way off and can almost place its progress by the rising and falling of its sound as it climbs hills and sinks down into the dips in the road. As it approaches, I quietly step off the road and step back a few feet into the surrounding trees. It passes by with its tail of dust like an antique metal road comet. There once was a car called the Peerless Road Incinerator because of the way it burned up the roads.

I always feel like an African when I do this, like a tribesman stepping off the road into the shadow of a giant philodendron as the oil company truck scoots by on some jungle track. In reality it's just Steve and Michelle from the south end, probably just coming up to get some gas for the boat, or they're out of butter or something. You sort of know what everyone is doing here, and it's kind of a drag.

The truck passes and I step out on the road again, walking through the dust that still hangs in the air. I come to the trail to Mark's, to the little green sward, grazed-down by sheep, that marks its entrance. It must have once been a logging road but now the forest has grown in on both sides. This land must have been fields at one time, open spaces that have now grown back in old alder. The alder trunks rise out of the salmon berry and sword fern like the white columns of a Greek

153

temple. In winter the trail is wet and mucky but today its clay is moist and pleasant to my bare feet. It feels good after the gravel and sharp rocks of Main road.

This feels like one of those days when I shouldn't have dropped: I've managed to be happy, not to think about Selene or Sheila or my daughter, but there is just too much pain building up in my body and I am frightened. I just want to be on the mountain, above the world, among wind twisted firs where sky-high ravens float in their golden psychedelic auras.

The trail comes out on the road that passes by the great old log house that Mark has patched up and taken over, the place where I spent my last night with Selene. Its original builders placed it up on the side of the hill where they could look over their fields. It is surrounded by an old orchard of twisted apple, plum and pear trees. Some of the pear trees tower over its battered shake roof. There is no smoke coming from the chimney, there is no sound. It looks like I am in luck today and nobody is home. I can slip quietly past the house into the old growth forest beyond. I decide to walk up past the house through the smooth grass rather than on the sharp gravel of the road.

As I walk past the house, marvelling at the huge tree trunks from which it was built, I see, too late, that Mark, Stewart and Curtis are in the back orchard.

Stewart is sitting on his horse, a roan gelding named Dutch. He has ridden under a transparent apple tree—the first ripe apples of summer—and is standing in the stirrups, pulling down yellow apples and tossing them down to Mark and Curtis. The tree glistens with highlights from the summer sun. Shafts of light pass through its branches and streak the man and horse underneath.

I think of diving back down the hill, but realise that it's too late: how strange that would look if they noticed me. So much pain and emotion is building in my body that the last thing I want to do is stand around and chat with everybody. How am I going to handle this? Mark and Curtis are laughing and pointing out apples that they can see from the ground. I think they are inviting Stew to stand up on the saddle to get some of the higher ones and he looks like he is about ready to take the dare, just to beat them at their own game. I decide to fake it, to say hello, to make conversation for a few minutes and then to continue on my way. If I stay any longer than that I'm afraid that I might start freaking out and have to say something pathetic like "I'm really stoned and scared." I might have to ask for help and I don't know if anyone is really up to it. The solitude of the forest is better.

I decide to be proactive. "Hey, be careful with them apples," I call out, imitating a harsh Mike voice. Mike always shows up in his ragged, half-rotten clothes and tells us how to do things, like he's some kind of big expert. All faces turn toward me, including Dutch's equine one. Dutch cants his head to one side to examine me with one great eye. They all get the joke and laugh. Mark tosses me an apple. It comes tumbling to me in a long golden arc like something out of mythology. The throw is so expert that I easily catch it. I take a bite, and get lost for a moment in its sweet juiciness, get lost in the whole idea of an apple tree, how it makes sweet food out of sunlight and earth. I think about how the tree spreads out above ground to catch air and light and below ground to catch water, minerals, and nourishment; about how at the end of the season it drops its leaves at its feet to reabsorb their nutrients. There is such Knowingness in this bite that I feel I have just eaten from the tree of knowledge.

Stewart looks benevolently down at me from Dutch's back. He is only twenty and has a ruddy face that glows with health and openness. He embodies the very bloom of youth. His young muscled body sits easily on the horse; his dark brown eyes are alive with merriment and friendliness. The whole scene is like a painting from another time. The Apple Pickers. I see it frozen for a moment, but then, in the silence of our greeting, a jet passes overhead, far away, in a series of deep distant rumbles that makes the canvas shimmer for a moment, reminding me that there is more to this moment than the simplicity that meets the eye.

We stand quietly for awhile eating these first apples of the year. Then Mark, whose place I am on, looks at me and says "What's happ'nin man?" Mark, like Stewart, is also really young. He has long, brown, kinky hair that he ties at the base of his neck, framing his soft dark face. He loves to joke and imitate voices and accents. He says this to me in a black southern accent. Mark knows how to take care of sick dogs and horses; he is willing to give them shots and stuff worm medicine down their throats.

"Not much," I say, "Just going up the mountain." Stewart looks up at the bright blue sky with a few eagles floating like specks in it. He says, "Nice day for it." He laughs his laugh, a big laugh of happy happenstance, a laugh that says, "isn't this great, you're going up the mountain and it's a nice day for it, and, hey, I'm here sitting on a horse, and isn't that also great."

"Far out," says Mark, "Going up to Alice in Wonderland. Too bad I gotta work on my house." He gestures at the house and, following his arm, I see the cedar shake-bolts that they have scrounged from the

beach, the hammer, the fro, the mallet cut from hawthorn, the steel wedges that sit on one of the shake-bolts. The grass is already littered with cedar scraps that will be gathered for kindling; there is a neat pile of shakes that have already been cut. I look up at the roof and see that there is a large hole open to the summer day. At the bottom of the hole there is already one row of bright cedar shakes that stand out sharply against the grey lichen covered ones on the rest of the roof. I realise that Curtis and Stewart have come to help Mark repair the hole in the roof that he kept a tarp tied over all last winter.

"Well," Curtis says, "maybe two of us should go up on the roof and one of us can stay down and keep the shakes coming." Curtis is a little older. He is lean in his sleeveless T-shirt, his long blond hair is tied at his neck and streaked with just a few strands of grey, a telltale sign that this is not really Eden. He is part of the commune—the good commune. He has built his own house on the land, and knows how to do these things, but he is tentative because it is really Mark's job and for him to organise.

A long technical conversation ensues—carried on through the munching of apples—as to whether the purlins are sound enough to take the new shakes. Inside me the pain is building and I begin to feel like I want to scream. We are standing in a row in front of and alongside Stewart and Dutch, all three of us, looking up at the roof. I am glad that I can just listen and not say anything, just look knowingly at the house and the pile of shakes. I am just containing everything that is building in me, waiting for my moment to say goodbye, when, suddenly, I feel a huge warm WHUMP across my back. Dutch has thumped me across the back with this neck, sending me stumbling out of line into the clearing. Curtis and Mark are pointing to the house, sketching something out with their fingers and don't notice but Stewart does. He laughs his accepting, embarrassed chuckle, and says, "easy Dutch." I turn around and look at Dutch. He is looking at me with one big round eye. He has caught my attention. I imagine he has picked up on my distress. I simply step back into line while the rest of the conversation about the roof goes on.

The discussion about rafters and purlins continues: "Maybe we could just nail some new poles next to the old ones to reinforce them and give the nails a little more to grab into. It would be a drag to have to take them all out. We could run up a few poles from the joists to support them." Young men with no old men to guide them are figuring it out together. Before alcoholism and then cancer took my father, when I was little, he did teach me how to use a hand saw, how to pick up nails around the house, how to hammer them into scrap 2X4's, how not to choke the hammer. After that he got too sick and just lay in bed all day, drunk on whiskey and stoned on Darvon, waiting for sunset, which he had come to love, writing poems in an unintelligible hand, poems that still sit in a shoe box at my sister's house, having defeated everyone's attempt at deciphering them. At least I got these small pieces from my father. The rest I had to figure out.

WHUMP! Dutch does it again, this time more gently. Stewart who is pointing to the roof line doesn't seem to notice. Dutch snorts a little. He looks at me again with his big eye and makes a little shake of his head. He jingles the bit in his mouth. I pat him on his neck, thinking that maybe that is what he wants, a perfunctory little pat, and I then step back in line again, feeling all this emotion inside me. Images of my daughter are rising before my eyes. My heart is bursting. I need the solitude of the forest, of being up on the slope of the mountain. I'm thinking of a way to leave casually that won't look like running into the forest. I'm trying to contain it, trying not to freak out.

I used to catch a ride down centre road and climb the mountain from the other side. It was so much easier to walk up that way. There is such a well worn groove, and it is also more beautiful as the logging of that side of the mountain has opened up the view. As I rose higher and higher there were great cliffs. Each stop for breath revealed more of the island, its forests, lakes and fields, of the surrounding islands, of the whole magnificent landscape, of far away Vancouver that looks like a lot of tiny plastic cubes scattered at the foot of the mountains.

Vancouver is really so small. With the exception of the clear-cuts, human habitation is really so insignificant. Every time I go up the clear-cuts seem to have gotten bigger, like ring worm spreading out across the mountains. From the top of the mountain I can see the whole world, south to Vancouver, west to Vancouver Island, north to the great fang-like peak that rises out of Johnston strait, east to the Coast Mountains and Texada island, which I believe was courteously put there by God to hide the abomination of the pulp mill at Powell River, a sort of insular fig leaf covering the unmentionables. You can still see the plume of smoke rising over Texada, though.

The easy trail is an old skidder road where the logger-cowboys used to pull logs down from the mountain, driving faster than hell so the giant first growth logs wouldn't overtake them and run them down. Malcolm Lowry said the good thing about logging is that it opens up the view, lets us see out. The reason I don't go up that way anymore is because I have to pass through a valley of stumps. With no forest to provide moisture the whole mountain side dried out and became a vale of crumbling shifting scree. Only a little kinick-kinick still grows there and something called yerba santa in California—it's called something else up here— which my mother pointed out to me when she climbed the mountain with me once.

The stumps are still growing. Their lips curl inward trying to cover a wound that is too big to heal. Some of them cover themselves over completely like an amputated arm or leg, but they don't seem to be able to put out a new shoot: What is left is a great underground tree, living on for years without its head, without its needles, without its connection to sun and moon and stars. I've tried piercing this living growth lip with my pocket knife and sticking in a young fir tip, hoping the graft would take, but I have never been systematic enough to go back and see if it worked. The I-Ching says Work On What Has Been Spoiled:

"The Chinese character Ku represents a bowl in whose contents worms are breeding...What has been spoiled through man's fault can be made good again through man's work. It is not immutable fate, as in the time of

162

Standstill, that has caused the state of corruption, but rather the abuse of human freedom."

Maybe, that's all we are doing, a whole generation of us, cleaning out the maggots. The valley of the broken trees is incredibly sad. It always reminds me of my father, reminds me that he was decimated and cut down before his time. When I'm stoned it feels too dark there—almost unbearable. I seem to have to sit on one of the still living stumps and feel this before I can move on. I look out to where Seattle is just a cloud of yellow smoke to the south, and I think of Sheila, and the blighted love we've always had for each other despite how things worked out. The curve of the Earth arches up between us like a woman's belly, and I think about the belly-up ocean of our troubles; about my daughter being so far away. I hope she is all right. I think she is. Little by little Peter is becoming her father. She scarcely knows me anymore. The broken forest evokes all this. That's why I don't go up that way anymore.

The way I go nowadays is all under forest. There is no view until the wonderful surprise at the top. As the acid comes on, I am usually past the trail; have entered the forest. It is uncharted, unmapped like the parts of myself that I am opening. I find my way through it differently each time. I have come to recognise certain parts of it as way stations, certain bluffs, certain moss clad rocks that I greet as friends and where I pause to enjoy the spirit of the place.

The forest is alive with mystery. Animal souls pass softly around me. Frozen by my presence, their soft brown eyes greet me as I come into their world without a gun, without intent to hurt. The deer, the feral sheep, feel this and pass easily around me. The ravens tell of mystery. Their repeated sequences of caws and clicks pass information from bluff to bluff like a coded news network. If I am lucky, the call of an eagle will fall from above like silver coins tossed from heaven. Sometimes the forest is filled with the sound of great beating wings, sometimes the song of many birds. Light and Dark pass through the trees as the sun is alternately exposed and hidden by clouds that pass overhead like God's watery ruminations.

I am near bursting from this long train of thought, when WHUMP! Dutch brings me back to the moment with another stroke of his Zen Master's neck. I step forward, out of his way, but his neck follows me. He presses it gently against my back like an invitation. I turn and look at him, meet the one great eye that I can see, and in so doing the understanding comes clearly to me: "Lean on me human, my body is so big and strong that all your puny little pain is nothing to me. It's like a mosquito bite. Here, lean against me and I will take it for you. It is nothing."

Now I understand what all this neck thumping is about. There must have been a time when humans could hear the thoughts of animals without the benefit of drugs. I marvel at what is happening and lean back against his great warm neck, surrender myself to Dutch. As I do, I feel the whole cloud of physical and emotional pain drain into his great brown body, grief, remorse, hopelessness all vanish. I turn and look at Dutch and he meets my eye with his. I see that it's OK. My pain is gone and he nuzzles my hair.

I pat him for awhile and hug his neck. I go over to where the apples are gathered in Mark's shirt and give him one. His eye twinkles at me. The conversation about the roof has ended and I find an old Frisbee next to the house and toss it to Mark. We toss it around for awhile, playing catch like the kids we were, only a few years ago.

Far across the field Mark crouches low and sends the Frisbee flying high above my head. I see the faded yellow disk pass above me and I run backward with all my might toward the edge of the forest. I leap high and pull it down with one hand, and whirl around toward my

165

friends. There is whooping and shouting at my catch. I stop and look at my friends. Stewart on his horse, Curtis long and lean in his singlet, Mark dark and stocky, and Dutch himself, prancing and working his bit, excited by the game of Frisbee.

This is a good minute to leave on my journey. I toss the Frisbee toward Stewart. The throw is a little short and I watch for a moment as he gallops forward to catch it. Curtis and Mark's eyes are on the horse and rider and I simply step back into the trees to continue my journey. In my mind I simply disappear, vanish, like one of those elves you read about in fairy tales. I am off to the forest!

XII
Maya

Maya and Ryan met on a B.C. Ferry. It was almost winter; already dark at 5 p.m. Since Selene left, Ryan had been living alone. When his mind turned toward Selene he simply moved it elsewhere. He was leaving her behind.

He had been self-sufficient, just happy to be on his own. He was living simply; doing yoga in the morning; refraining from drugs and alcohol; truly celibate. He was relieved to be free of the entanglements of desire and attraction and not wanting to be plunged back into samsara again. He was returning from one of those supply trips to Vancouver, hitchhiking again, his huge pack filled with brown rice, a gallon can of sunflower oil, some figs, a block of cheese, a bag of flour, fresh tofu from the Sunrise Market, a can of peanut butter.

On the ferry, Maya and he recognised each other as being from the same tribe by the colourful patched clothes and hand-knit caps they were both wearing. It was easy to speak. She carried a guitar and played it for him. It seemed like one of those chance, intense, short meetings that happened so frequently in those days; that both of them would soon be whirled away in their separate directions never to meet again.

The Queen of Tsawwassen crossed the dark waters of Georgia Strait looking like a floating city of light. A medieval mystic once compared human life to a swallow flying out of the winter darkness, through an open window, into a warmly lit church; then flying out the opposite window, back into darkness. That was how it was: they felt that they only had those fleeting moments of connection out on the late autumn waters. Huddled in their corner, surrounded by the polyester clad denizens of the other side, they made the best of it.

She said she was going to Hornby, another of the gulf islands. He was going to Vasquez. As the ferry pulled in, they went their separate ways, each walking through the car deck, tapping on windows and asking drivers if they could give them a ride north to where each of them had to catch their next ferry This worked much better than anonymously hitching on the dark open road. Later, when Ryan grew old, he remembered this time and wondered at the chutzpah of his younger self. He realised that now he could never do this. He would worry too much about imposing on people. Perhaps, he thought, it had been his youth, his charm, an unconscious knowledge of his own young beauty that had made it possible.

He got a ride through the pouring rain all the way to the boat basin. The rain lashed down and a southeast gale howled through the rigging of the fish boats. Running with his heavy pack through the downpour to the wharf, drenched in spite of his rain gear, he climbed into the rusty cabin of the ferry. On board, people were passing a bottle back and forth to fortify themselves for the shit-kicking that they knew they were going to get. Several people got off the boat, deciding to stay with friends in town rather than make the crossing.

At the very last minute Maya came bouncing aboard the ferry. He was astounded at her arrival and rose to welcome her. The ferry's diesel engine roared, the wooden bar was shoved into the brackets on the double doors. The boat plunged out into the dark night.

Maya was diminutive but her eyes were full of light. Rain cascaded down her face from the soaked hand-knit cap that was tied beneath her chin. Her light brown hair hung out from under it in soaked strings. The cap was of natural wool, its yellow stripes had been dyed with onion peels. People saved onion peels in buckets under the sink to give to their weaver friends. She came and sat with him on the sagging blanket covered couch. She was shivering. She told him that she

169

had just decided to get off at Vasquez to see what it was like; to come to the dance at the Legion hall that he had told her about on the big ferry. She had just asked her ride to let her off at the boat basin. It was clear to him that she had followed him aboard. It seemed like a little miracle. He had been taken with her too.

They were both drenched and so cold that he took the blanket off the couch and wrapped it around them. He invited her to stay with him and she accepted. Then the Captain Vancouver left the riprap and was hit by the full force of the gale. As the first wave hit, the boat tilted and wallowed. The diesel engine roared as the propeller lifted from the water. The old couches began to slide back and forth across the boot-wet floor. Maya and Ryan leaned back into the wet tattered couch and closed their eyes. They were like lost children, unparented, trying to find a real life, trying to be adults, in the world that they had created in the abandoned homesteads along the coast. They had learned how to comfort each other. He put his arm around her and held her as they crossed the great waters. She put her hand in his. It was as simple as that in this world of magic and illusion. In Sanskrit her name, Maya, meant "the divine dance," the play of the gods that forms this illusory world.

Within days they were clear that this was "the one," by which they meant the relationship that would last their whole life and heal the woundings from all their other relationships. Wearing their knitted wool caps and carrying their big packs, they traveled north to Hornby Island, to make this joyous announcement to her married friends, who simply replied "we hope so," without, Ryan thought, too much enthusiasm in their voices.

They stayed in her little cabin in Ford's Cove, a small valley full of shack-like cabins whose fences were collapsing from the weight of mounded blackberry vines. During the day they walked the trails of the island. It was an ecstatic time; the last clear days of autumn were declining into winter; the maple branches were bare with only a few yellow flags left flying. There were alternate days of sunshine and rain. The forest floor was blanketed with great piles of brown maple leaves. He imagined hibernating there; just heaping up a huge pile of leaves under the arch of a cliff and then climbing into it to sleep away the winter.

They shared their whole lives on this trip together, their histories, their learnings. They told each other about their ex-husbands and wives, about lovers and sexual experiences. She taught him meditation. Somehow they were both ready to find a path of peace in the swirling storm of relationship. They read Suzuki Roshi to each other and talked about their practices, about beginner's mind, about gaining ideas. Autumn continued its slow decline into winter until the branches were completely bare and the sky was as hollow and empty as a Zen master's mind. Still they didn't return to his farm, living tucked away in her little cabin.

He made friends with Zach, the man who lived in the cabin next door. When Maya was meditating in the morning, he went over to his cabin; drank tea and had a toke with him. Zach lived alone and was self-contained and happy. His bachelor cabin was immaculate. At night he sat by his table and carved or played music. He worked for a local farmer during the day, spreading fertilizer in winter, turning the soil and planting in spring, weeding and harvesting in summer and autumn. He had slightly curly shoulder length brown hair, a pleasant open face, and clear direct blue eyes. One morning he told Ryan about an experience with fate. He had come to Hornby to live alone and had spent many months just working the fields during the day and playing his guitar at night. During that time he was not lonely, just happy with what he had and glad to live each day for what it was. And then one night at sunset, sitting on the porch playing his guitar, he thought, "Lord I am lonely; I am ready for a relationship now."

Half an hour later, just as the land was settling into twilight monochrome, a figure came up the dark road to his bachelor cabin, just a shadow at first, then emerged into a woman carrying a pack and a guitar case. They had met long ago while travelling, and he had told her that he lived on Hornby. She had carried him in her memory all this time and decided to find him. She only knew his first name and had needed to ask around until someone knew where he lived. Now she was there.

Zach made them tea and they played their guitars and sang together on the porch. The darkness gathered around them; crickets played their tiny chimes into the summer night. She stayed through autumn and all of winter. His desire for a relationship was granted half an hour after the wish was made.

In the spring she left to work at planting strawberries in Saanich. They had loved lightly, seemingly without the deep emotions that always arose for Ryan. They parted easily. Their relationship was more like a sexual sadhana, their parting like a simple bow to a teacher.

The I Ching, hexagram 61, Chung Fu/ Inner Truth, says:

Six in the third place means:
He finds a comrade.
Now he beats the drum, now he stops.
Now he sobs, now he sings.

Richard Wilhelm, in his commentary, remarks:

Here the source of a man's strength lies not in himself but in his relation to other people. No matter how close to them he may be, if his centre of gravity depends on them, he is inevitably tossed to and fro between joy and sorrow. Rejoicing to high heaven and then sad unto death—this is the fate of those who depend on an inner accord with other persons whom they love. Here we have only the statement of the law that this is so. Whether this condition is felt to be an affliction or the supreme happiness of love, is left to the subjective verdict of the person concerned.

Writing this, as an old man, Ryan spends the morning searching for this hexagram in his old copy of the *I-Ching*. Its yellow cover is smudged with woodsmoke. Its spine is broken, the ghost of the scotch tape that once held it together is imprinted on its ragged edges. He finds the small envelope that as a young man

174

he had pasted in the back cover. It still holds the three Chinese coins needed to throw the oracle. On the backside of the fold-out chart used to find the hexagram that one has thrown, are the crude pencil rubbings of the back and front of a coin, labelled "heads" and "tails." Ryan had made them so that he could remember which was which. The Chinese coins made it difficult to know which end was up.

Ryan also sees the numerical values he had recorded for the coins. The inscribed side is worth 2, un-inscribed (tails) is worth three. There is also a sample of the possible combinations. It looks like this:

6— x —
7 — —
8 ———
9 —0—

He remembers: the broken lines are yin and the solid lines yang. The lines with the x's and o's indicate lines that change into their opposite polarity to create a new hexagram. They show what the current situation will evolve into. Yin at its extreme changes into yang and vice versa.

Ryan is flabbergasted to recall that for several years he had used this oracle to make all his decisions; that he had sat by the fire and puzzled out what the cryptic lines might mean for him. Or did it make his decisions? Were the lines so cryptic and inscrutable that, ultimately, he had been left to decide for himself what they meant? Perhaps—once again—it just came down to him: that while believing in god, in the oracle, in synchronicity, he had simply made a bunch of choices that now he lived with.

Many of Zach and Ryan's conversations were about synchronicity and the manifestation of thoughts in material reality. Zach told him about sitting in the local pub one night, watching a local landowner buy drinks for the house to the drunken cheers and acclaim of those around him. The landowner had logged large portions of the island, stripped it, sold it for subdivisions, and screwed almost everyone in the process. All this seemed forgotten in the alcoholic largesse of his ill gained wealth.

Zach, who had the money for two beers, sat sipping the last one and wondered to himself: "Dear God, how is it that I try so hard and have so little and he is doing so well when he has violated everything and everyone." Instantly, as if in answer to Zach's question, the land owner turned red in the middle of a toast and keeled apoplectically over. He lay on the floor clutching his chest, his face contorted in terror, his eyes rolling

176

with fear. He shit and pissed himself and desperately tried to say something but only slurred word salad came out. No one touched him. They stood in a circle around him wondering what to do. Everyone stepped back from the puddle on the floor. Zach moved through the circle, an unwanted hippy in this circle of island rednecks. He pushed his way through, realising that the man was not just drunk, but that something was seriously wrong. He got to the front just in time to see him die, but not in time to take the desperately extended hand that reached out for comfort only to grasp thin air. To Zach his question has been answered in a most terrible way. He had been shown that on Earth crime pays, but that when it comes to facing eternity, such a life has cultivated little with which to face it.

It was wet raining winter when Maya and Ryan returned to Ryan's homestead on Vasquez. Maya had turned her cabin over to a friend, another single lady who lived on Hornby. When they arrived with their big packs, they saw the winter's wood that Ryan had cut in autumn. It was neatly stacked in the shed; the butt ends of the logs had turned the savage orange that alder becomes as it dries. The door was unlocked and they walked in. It was much as they had left it six weeks ago. There were a few notes on the table from people who had spent the night, thanking Ryan for the shelter. Ryan and Maya took off their packs and built the fires together.

Things went well at first. They even worked together to help Selene through her operation. But with time Maya became disturbed by Ryan's excessive drinking and drugging. She began trying to rein him in a little, to move him back toward the vegetarian food and the pure life style that had been his when they met. A power struggle ensued that quickly eroded their ecstasy and passion. Though they were kindly expressed, Ryan felt oppressed by Maya's strictures. He decided that it wouldn't work. He asked her to leave. It had only been a few months.

XIII
Alone On The Farm

After that, Ryan was alone on the farm; Maya and Selene were long gone; winter had passed slowly; spring was approaching. Overhead the sky clicked into a different notch.

On nights when the Northeaster's clear winds had laid the clouds to rest, the late winter constellations burned overhead—Orion, Draco, Perseus, Aquarius, Pisces. It was as though the mythical star beings had disassembled the clouds and spread their frozen droplets in a thin crystal quilt on the ground. The silver-frost covered the field, the tree tops, the roof, the entire sleeping world. The moon lit its myriad tiny crystals, making the landscape look like it was made of glass. When morning came the frost vanished like magic, drawn back up to heaven.

When Ryan stepped out to pee at night, he now saw a light glimmering out of the old house down the road that had been empty for so long. It was comforting to have neighbors living in his little valley. While he had been on Hornby, Feather and Jim had moved in. They were both carvers. She had long red hair and he had long black hair.

Feather had just finished apprenticing to be a shipwright. One day she made a slip of the tongue and said that she had "apprenticed to be a Smithright." Smithright was the name stencilled on all the garbage bins up and down the Fraser. She laughed and acknowledged that sometimes, as a woman breaking into a male trade, it had felt like she was apprenticing to be a garbage bin: she had been given all the shit work such as applying poisonous wood preservatives down in the cramped bilges of fish boats. Now that she had survived her apprenticeship, she planned to make her living by repairing wooden boats out on the islands. Ryan surmised that she was called Feather because of the easy lightness she embodied.

Jim was a young Haida man, sculpted and aristocratically so, with very fine straight long black hair. His name was really Sandy Jim, his last name having been taken from the first name of his village's missionary. Everybody called him Indian Jim, not maliciously, but to distinguish him from Stump Farm Jim, Tractor Jim, and South End Jim. Except for Jim it was a first name culture. Nobody called him Sandy.

During Feather's apprenticeship, Jim had been able to stand the city, along with the hundred years of destruction that it had rained on his people, because he understood it to be a short term phenomenon; a brightly lit bubble on the waters of time.

The old ways had almost died at the hands of fervent Protestants, who Jim thought of as having, in a rare spirit of ecumenism, continued the work of the Spanish Inquisition. They had taken away the children—his parents—and forbade them to speak their own language; they had banished the implements of magic and the ceremonies of give-away that had held their culture together; they had impregnated the people with smallpox, alcohol and syphilis. The children had been tortured in forbidding buildings called "Residential Schools," which in their gloom and sorrow reminded Jim more of Dachau and Bergan-Belsen. His parents had told him that speaking their own language had been punished by beatings, humiliation, sexual abuse, and deprivation of food (if it could even have been called that). Jim wondered why Canadians bothered to hunt down old Nazis when similar criminals could be found right at home with less expense to the taxpayer.

Over many years, the children of the "Residential Schools" had found their way home. The thread of the past had been torn but not completely broken. Many old

181

grannies remembered the way. Many old grannies kept their doors open as their broken children returned from having been eaten by this foreign D'sonoqua, this Moloch, this Whore of Babylon. Hedges of broken trucks and crumbling houses provided the privacy needed for expelling the poisons of genocide; releasing the evil spirits gathered in the belly of the goddess of death. Their enemies thought that nothing important could be happening in such squalor, but they were wrong. In Haida Gwaii they were building a new Big House, the first in a long time. Jim knew that when he had children of his own, they would learn the language and the old ways.

Feather and Jim had taken over the just barely standing house, and also its broken down barn. The barn was not a barn as you might think of a barn, but simply a low shed made with flimsy fir poles covered by shakes. Feather had patched the roof, stapled plastic over the empty window frames, put in a tin heater and was using it to build a dory.

Between them, Feather and Jim owned a formidable collection of chisels. From the outside, their relationship looked like it was mostly about chisels. Both in the house and barn, there were always long curls of yellow cedar floating around them, like Rapunzel's hair. They were always sharpening chisels by sliding them over whetstones slurried with oil. There were big chisels, little chisels, odd shaped chisels, V shaped chisels, U shaped chisels, ones with strange compound curves. They appraised the effectiveness of their sharpening work by testing the edges of their chisels on their thumbs, which they often cut. They went through lots of Band-Aids. There were always bloody Kleenexes on the floor along with the wood curls.

In their house there was a hand-crank phonograph left over from the thirties, and the collection of seventy-eight records that went with it. There were also old plates, pots and pans, ancient beds and bedsprings, moth-eaten chenille bedspreads, all left from long ago. The old lady who grew up in the house had moved to a little trailer in False Bay. The trailer had propane heat, and it was easier for her to live there. When Feather went to pay the twenty five dollar a month rent, she was always invited in for tea. Once, when she noticed that all the plants in the old lady's trailer were dying, she asked her, "What's wrong with the plants?"

The old lady said, "They don't seem to like the propane heat. It just seems to kill them." Feather, adjusting her tone to be as friendly and non-confrontational as possible, asked: "Well, what do you think it's doing to you?" The old lady just laughed uncomfortably, and settled back into her one great chair.

Ryan took to visiting Feather and Jim in the evenings. A visit usually entailed drinking some of Feather's genteel fruit wine, Old Lady Wine, was what she called it. Though young and fiery, Feather liked to make sweet cordials from the plums and blackberries she gathered. She served them in the antique etched glasses that she had found in the house's cupboard. Ryan sat talking while sorting through the old 78's. He'd pick one to put on, crank up the phonograph and they'd listen to the scratchy cowboy music. He watched Feather and Jim sit in their chairs and sharpen chisels, Jim with his long black hair, and Feather with her long red hair. Each of them had their own kerosene lamp on a table next to them. There was always a certain amount of pride when they cut themselves. "Owww, God Damn, that's sharp!"

The whole slump-roofed building, its flowered wallpaper, its wood cookstove, its hand-crank phonograph, the great honeysuckle mounding on its roof, was like a stage set from another time, a left over, complete with furnishings. Time and the tide, as well as waiting for no man, don't seem to pass by all at once: they both leave little puddles, tide pools or time pools, sanctuaries where stranded sea life (and people), can live while time and tide flow impatiently around them.

Even though Ryan's friends and he were trying to be more like natives, trying to create something of a tribe out on the island, mostly they had only read about them in books. The only time Ryan had actually been around natives, before getting to know Jim, was during a stint at the herring cannery in Bamfield. He remembered wading all day long in his rubber overalls and boots through tonnes of silvery fish, squeezing the pink roe out of them and placing the ovaries in buckets of brine. About half of the people working in the cannery were natives. There was one beautiful woman who went home at night with her father and husband in an ancient dugout canoe equipped with a modern outboard motor. On one of Ryan's many unintended days off, when there were no fish, Ryan had walked past their house on his way to a beach. Only its shake roof was visible above the mounds of blackberries and leafy tops of fruit trees. He heard her singing to a baby deep inside the old wood structure, hidden from his prying eyes, hidden from the culture that had left them only this small sliver of land by the sea, all that remained of the vast reaches they had once watched over.

The same week another native woman gave birth to a child and none of the native workers showed up for three days. To them a birth was cause for celebration and celebrate they did, much to the disgust of the managers of the now short-staffed cannery.

It was hard to get to know the native people. Whites, mostly old timers, hippies, and natives all kept to their own kind. At one point Ryan, overcame his shyness and struck up a conversation with the older native man who drove the fork lift. They stood in their hard hats and talked about herring roe. He told Ryan that he thought "the Japanese ate it for some special kind of holiday, like the Canadians eat turkey at Thanksgiving or those Japanese oranges at Christmas." Ryan noticed that he said "Canadians." He did not say "We."

The attempt at conversation soon faltered and they just stood for a moment in the early morning sun, in their rubber overalls and hard hats, and looked at each other. Ryan felt transparent, as though all the stuff that he hid from the world was spilled out on his shirt like breakfast egg. Ryan had heard that Orcas couldn't hide, that their sonar way of "seeing" let them look right through each other; let them perceive the knotted belly, the tensions in each other's body; that it was all in the open. That was how he felt with this quiet man. To Ryan's surprise, the man looked back at him with openness and acceptance. In that moment Ryan felt that he had been seen for the desperately flawed being that he was and that that was OK: there was no expectation for perfection; that his humanness, with its seed of divinity, outshone his flaws.

On another day Ryan overheard a native woman next to him talking to another woman about a party. She was telling about a woman who had gotten jealous and broken a bottle over another woman's head. What was interesting to Ryan, as he squeezed ovaries from the endless river of dead fish that spewed from the aluminum chute, was that there was none of the outrage that there would have been if this happened at a Canadian party. None of the ostracism. They said in their soft voices "It's too bad she lost control," but even this flawed act was viewed with melancholy compassion and an understanding that we are all humans, little clay golems running around and learning hard lessons. With such a long road ahead, it was better to be accepting and not hope for more than was reasonable.

The village of Bamfield is spread along both sides of an inlet. The inlet is the main street and people travel up and down it in boats. Small, old fashioned houses line the waterfront. The forest is behind them. On the far side of the inlet, a wooden boardwalk provides the means to get around on foot. The Japanese overseers lived in a small cabin they had rented on the boardwalk. During the day they stalked through the cannery in their rubber coveralls and hard-hats, giving orders to cannery foremen and workers in a language no-one could understand. The Canadians and Natives all thought they were making some headway in learning Japanese when they learned that certain unformed herring ovaries were called "imachalo" and went in a separate bucket. It was only weeks later, when the bucket was labelled in English, that they realised that the Japanese overseers had been speaking English all along; that imachalo was simply how they said "immature roe." On days off, when Ryan walked past their house on the boardwalk, he saw their shoes and gum boots placed neatly, two by two, on the porch outside the door. He imagined that after hot baths, in place of the onsen, they had changed into clean clothes and enjoyed small amenities that they had brought to this wild land from their old refined culture. He imagined that behind the walls of their cabin they had created a small place of refuge.

Occasionally a seaplane flew in and elegant Japanese people dressed in suits and wearing gold jewellery stepped like Asian princes onto the floating dock. The overseers of the overseers. The local ones always rushed down to the dock and greeted them with repeated bows. Then they took them through the cannery where the higher-ups viewed the Canadian workers with an aloof, arms-length disdain.

One night on Vasquez, lonely in his cabin, Ryan had picked some vegetables from the garden and taken them down to have dinner with Feather and Jim. While they were working to prepare dinner, Jim and Ryan joked about each other's food.

"How can you stand to spread that fishy oolichan grease your mother sends you on your toast?"

"Yeah, well, I don't know how white people eat avocados: Ugh, they are green and slimy."

As they were chopping the vegetables, Ryan entertained them with the story of how he had heard Mt. St. Helens blow. "I had been in my front yard, fitting a new handle into an old axe head. It was the day of the Victoria Day picnic and I had already put on my good clothes. I was doing something I could do without getting dirty. Suddenly a shock wave passed over from far away and echoed back again from the bluff behind the house. BOOM! Then it happened again. BOOM! I thought, 'Somebody must be blasting stumps down at the south end.' I waited for another blast, but none came so I went back to my axe handle, wondering who could be blasting that day.

"Later, when I walked into the picnic, a biker named Bill came up and said "Hey man, did you hear Mt. St. Helens blow this morning?" Everyone was

189

talking about how the mountain—300 miles away— had blown its top with such force that everyone on the island had heard it.

"It was several days later that Seam and I had decided to drive my Epic Envoy down I-5 to see the aftermath. Seam was a Sitar player. He was a dropped-out musicologist who made me a chart that showed every modal scale known to man. It all fit onto one piece of paper. I used to carry it around everywhere. I didn't really understand it, but, like, it was so far-out, so intricate and complex, that it seemed like a talisman, a magical key that would unlock any secret that the musical universe might throw at me."

"Seam and I got as far as southern Washington. The highway was so full of swirling white ash that it was frightening. We couldn't even see the brake lights of cars twenty feet in front of us. Humungous trucks loomed up out of the whiteness and leaned on the horn. There was really nothing to see. It was just a blizzard of ash." Ryan took his chopped vegetables and placed them in a bowl next to the cook stove.

"Far out, we didn't hear it," Feather said, heating oil in a pan, "In Richmond there's just too much happening, machines roaring, planes taking off and landing at the airport, trucks rumbling by, boats churning up and down the Fraser."

"Yeah," Ryan offered, "the radio said that the blast was equal to that of a 2 megaton hydrogen bomb."

His remark fell into silence. Everybody chopped and grated. He had the feeling that he had said something offensive. He was always worried about saying the wrong thing to people of different races. Even more troubling was that sometimes he unconsciously started imitating their accents. Finally, it was Jim who spoke. He had moved from dicing the zucchini to paring the apples for the crumble they were going to have for desert. Without looking up he said, "Yeah, they're always comparing the forces of nature to their own little toys."

That elegant, exclusive "they" again.

When Ryan walked back up the road to his house that night, plum wine, conversation and old cowboy music had left him uplifted and hopeful. He looked at the constellations. He did not know the name of most of them. In the midst of the spring chill, frogs had already reawakened to fill parts of the night with their rhythmic chanting.

Earlier in the evening, holding glasses of plum wine, Ryan, Feather and Jim had stood out on the porch listening to the frogs. They had looked up at the stars and debated whether or not it was worthwhile to know their names; whether it added something or took something away. "Why not just look at them in awe and amazement? Why activate the mind. Why say Orion, Pleides, Leo, Aquarius? We have tried that before, look where it's gotten us." They had gone back inside and continued the argument. More plum wine had been poured. This was the sort of thing that they talked about seriously.

On the road home it was silent. The moon lit the ice-dust world. The translucent star-beings had come down and must have been wandering through the woods. A different page had turned. The women Ryan had loved were gone. He was alone again. In this he could feel his individuality, his own little spark of life burning in the midst of the heavenly fires around him.

XIV
Snartch

It was around this time, that Hirsh and Snartch came to Vasquez to stay with Ryan. Several weeks later Hirsh went to Victoria to pick up his unemployment cheque and left Snartch with Ryan. Hirsh's trip also involved visiting friends, pubbing, getting laid, buying dope and other necessities. He was gone for several days during which the dog slunk around, uncomfortable at being left with a stranger. Snartch's hip dysplasia had become much worse. At best he hobbled around in a permanent cringe. Aside from his deformity, he was always looking over his shoulder with a hangdog expectation of being hit or reprimanded. He was not a pleasant dog.

Taking advantage of Hirsh's absence, Ryan dropped acid one day and was amazed at the strangeness of the dog. It had an abnormally long nose and droopy eyes and looked like it had just slid out of a Breugel canvas. Ryan and the dog stared at each other in mutual amazement at each other's strangeness.

In his expanded state, Ryan needed to get out of the confines of the house. Taking pity on Snartch, he invited him along. Snartch hobbled slowly after Ryan, cringing all the way, as though Ryan were taking him out to sacrifice him to Jehovah. It took much encouragement and gentle-voiced coaxing just to get Snartch to limp along.

They went up over the hill past what was now called Smedley's—formerly The Old Walsh place —and into the flowing fields beyond. Smedley's cabin was always empty and locked; sometimes, as he walked past, Ryan had fantasies of ghosts or of a little old dead lady living inside. Under the penetrating light of the drug, he could see that it was just an old house inhabited by nothing but his imagination. Wood returning to earth. He laughed at its simplicity and innocence.

Behind the house, in the open fields, it was a Van Gogh sort of day. The brown grass swirled and flowed. The leaves of the cattails bent and danced in the wind. The fir branches were bent to the curve of the great wheel that moved through everything. The drug allowed Ryan to see that Snartch didn't need to be as crippled as he was; that his deformity was an adaptation to cruelty; that he had moulded his life around living off crumbs of sympathy rather than enjoying the equality of fun and companionship.

Ryan walked over to Snartch and squatted beside him. For the first time he felt genuine affection for this monstrosity of a dog. He laughed at his affliction, at his camouflage, and patted him warmly, roughing him up and playing with him a bit. He got a stick and held it until Snartch opened his mouth and tugged at it a little: the world's smallest stick game. By now Ryan was a funnel of energy. The drug had removed some impediment and allowed the universes electricity to flow freely through him. He energised this game, filled it with truth and reality until even Snartch, hang-dog Snartch, began to feel that it was true. Snartch growled and pulled back on the stick, trying to wrest it from Ryan's hand.

Ryan started throwing the stick, just a little way at first, one or two feet, and then raced Snartch to see if Snartch could get there first. Snartch rose to the occasion. Soon Ryan was throwing the stick ten, twenty, thirty, then fifty feet; racing the dog for it. Snartch moved faster and faster. Soon Ryan was hurling the stick in great end-over-end parabolas out across the grass and cattails. Snartch and he ran and bounded after it like tiny figures in a huge Rousseau landscape. Gone was the hip dysplasia. Gone was the cringe. Snartch bounded effortlessly after the stick; leapt gracefully in the air to catch it in mid flight. He held it in his mouth and fiercely dodged Ryan's attempts to get it. They walked the long valleys together, past the Valley House, into the long flowing fields behind it, running and leaping in the tall grass. The late afternoon sun slanted up the valley from the islands coast, lighting everything sideways, illuminating the grass, illuminating the fir trees that seemed to watch like elders from the sides of the valley. Ryan ran and sweated. Running with this animal, he delighted in his own animal physicality.

They turned to go home, running, leaping, jumping until they approached Smedley's, where Ryan could see the mould beginning to take hold of Snartch again. The dog began to slow down, cringe a bit and hang behind. He limped after the stick now and by the time they reached Ryan's house, Snartch had settled back into the crippled hangdog he had always been. The trip didn't last. Even dogs wore mind-forged manacles it seemed.

Ryan remembered a couple that he and Sheila had met when they were camping in New Brunswick. The couple had told them about visiting Nantucket Island and meeting the Village Idiot there. They said that he had turned out to be just a person of somewhat limited intelligence, who would have passed for normal or slightly dull anywhere else. But on an island, having his so called idiocy reflected to him by everyone around, he had taken on the role and lived a limitation far below his actual ability. It was expected of him.

Ryan felt himself coming down as well, settling into rebirth, losing the infinite freedom of the realms of energy. Slowly he settled back into his own mould of limitation, the resentments, petty jealousies, fears, and worries that kept him from enjoying the gift of life; the pain of it, he thought, was enough to turn you into a Buddhist. Then he remembered what Selene had told him "You don't come down completely. A small fraction of the experience is retained each time."

That night Hirsh came back, worn out from a weekend of pubbing and screwing. He was very good, very confident about picking up women. He fed Snartch, and Snartch hobbled to his bowl, looking soulfully over his shoulder at Ryan before beginning to eat. Did he remember? Hirsh and Ryan sat at the round table and had an ordinary conversation, carefully polishing the links of their mind-forged manacles in the evening lamplight.

XV
Who Was This Ryan?

Who was this Ryan who seemed to enjoy his life so much while making such a bad job of it? For two chapters he got to speak for himself, a voice from the past, a historically trumped up reconstitution of Ryan, a simulacrum of who I might have been back then. So, why can't I, the old man who is writing this, who is bringing Ryan back to life, who's jerking the strings so he can dance on stage again, speak for myself too, instead of slithering around behind the scenes, speaking through the voices of these characters?

Who was this Ryan who made all those decisions which I spend my waning years trying to rectify? Who was he and who was he becoming? Was he becoming me? Am I a wiser, more loving person now? Was there some good that came out of all of this?

I wonder how we lived through all of those events, the twists, the turns, the mistakes, the passionate loves, and the injury to each other, the bad decisions, the split up families, the living out the unfortunate consequences.

How did we do all this living before we were even twenty five, with no elders to guide us, perhaps only a few voices from books, subject to our misinterpretation?

All of this for a few moments of joy, of creation, of insight, of understanding, of ecstasy, of real love, of sacrifice, of caring. All this for a few moments that stand out in memory, and, between these bright moments, the great dark form of living. Regret. We try to guide our children so they won't have regret. The path of least regret. We learn about forgiveness from the spiritual traditions, particularly self-forgiveness.

One night, in Sooke, the city where I have been living for many years, there is a knock on my door. I am sitting in the living room watching TV and drinking a glass of wine. Usually at this hour it is someone collecting for Greenpeace or selling hand-painted cards that I buy a couple of—because I believe in supporting initiative and artistic endeavour—and then never use because they just don't have enough artistic interest to send to someone (I mean, like, I don't want any of my friends to think that this is my taste in art). I leave my wine glass on the coffee table and go to get the door.

A woman, in her sixties, face weathered and beautiful, eyes laughing as if at some secret joke, stands silently before me. I look at her and see something so familiar about her. I feel whole areas of my brain being mobilised. Something neurologically immense is happening. I look at her, trying to integrate her features. What is it about this stranger that leaves me reeling and speechless, eyes glued to her eyes, no words coming? Suddenly the word comes. The pattern of her face snaps into a gestalt and I see Selene standing before me: "Selene!"

This is a mystery of mysteries, what is she doing standing at my door, after all these years? I invite her in. She tells me she got a phone message from me, several weeks ago, asking her to call. She was in town visiting Clive, a mutual friend who lives just two blocks away. He told her that I lived nearby and she just decided to come over rather than phone.

I invite her in and offer her wine, which she declines but accepts some juice. I am totally puzzled about this mysterious phone call that I never made. Finally, after much hashing and rehashing—Selene and I always liked to sleuth things out—it comes to me that I had left a message for another woman to call me with regards to a class I was teaching. I had not known that the number she had left me was Selene's number; that she had been staying at Selene's house in Duncan. The woman had not been there and I remembered that someone else had taken down the message. They had forgotten to put the woman's name on it and the message had gotten confused. Selene found the message on her message pad—call Ryan 250 646-9889—and wondered why I wanted her—after all these years—to call!

That figured out, we sit down and make small talk. I introduce her to my wife, Cora, who says "hi," and discretely leaves. I tell her about my life as a teacher and she tells me about hers as an ethnobotanist. "I'm working on First Nations land claims, helping to authenticate them. I drive out to the west coast a lot, to Tofino and Ucluelet"

Whatever happened between us, happened in that moment of recognition at the door. Our history has been swirled away by our lives and the intervening years. The poems we wrote to each other, all the relationship confusion, her healing me with her hands, the plastic house in the woods, the pain of our separation, are still alive in my memory and I assume in hers too. We don't speak of it, though. We speak of the present. It is like choosing to live in present day Rome rather than in its awful catacombs, rather than in the dreadful significance of the past. And that which is called love, the terrible bond that holds two together, in surrender or in struggle, is gone; not there; only a memory. Heart connection, passion, lust, jealousy, fear, adventure, desire, attachment, need, no longer exist between us. We are just two old people sitting in chairs talking to each other.

After she left I remembered hitchhiking on a snowy day up to the hospital in Cumberland, a little mining town above Courtenay, where Selene was having her surgery. When I was rid of her, when I had cleansed my mind of her and was with Maya, she suddenly out of the blue called from Oregon. She left a message with one of the few people on the island who had a phone, asking me to call. When I called her back, her voice was small and frightened and far away.

"*I've been doing a lot of thinking,*" *she said.* "*I realize that things were pretty crazy with us before I left. That night at Mark's, you said you wished there was something you could do to get me to change my mind. There's no need to do anything. It's about me. I wonder if you still want to get together. I've decided I do want to get together, to get married.*"

I was silent for a long time. "*I have met someone.*"

"*Is it serious?*"

"*Yes, I think so.*

There was another long pause in which neither of us talked. The phone hissed softly as though the line was

202

travelling across empty miles of blowing blizzard. I thought about Maya cooking our dinner at home, and the start that we had made. About how intoxicated we were about living our lives together. I thought about the days of letting Selene go and how I had turned my mind away from her whenever I found myself thinking of her. In the three months that Selene had been gone, I had freed myself from her, and from the confusing, sticky life I had led with her. I felt like I was in a normal relationship again, although Maya had already said something about "I don't want to become a closed off little couple, I want to be able to share the love we have with other people and renew our love in that way." I had decided, for my own peace of mind, not to ask exactly what she meant by this. I had decided that it just must mean that she wanted us to have lots of friends, not to become closed off and insular. I wondered if anything would be different if Selene and I went back together or would we just fall into old ways of being.

It felt to me like that machine that Selene and I had experienced on mushrooms; that she and I were just on different bounces: now that she was ready to commit, I had moved on and was with another woman. I wondered, with the magical thinking that is still part of me, if it was just not meant to happen between Selene and I; if it was meant to happen—for both of us—in

another way; which it did. Fate again. The answer, my
sad answer coming out of the long silence on the hissing
line, was "I can't go back."

Two weeks later she called again. I slogged down
the dirt road in the rain to return her call. I held the
phone into the corner to have some privacy in the noisy,
child-filled house of my neighbors.

"What's up," I said?

"I have a problem. Some kind of uterine growth
inside me. I'm so scared."

"What? What happened? How do know?"

"I wasn't feeling right and went to a friend's
doctor for a check up. He felt something in my abdomen
and sent me for some kind of scan. He called me in for
the results and said that there was some kind of growth
in me. I just got this rush of fear and now it's with me all
the time."

"What is it?"

"They're not sure. They say I have to have it out.
Then they will biopsy it. I'm scared.
I'm coming back to have it done in BC. I can't afford to
have it done down here. I know you don't want to get
back together, but I'm wondering if you will help me
through this."

I didn't know what to say. I was at a loss. The hissing line again. Finally she said, "are you still there?"

"Yes," I said, "I can help you."

Selene came to the island and stayed with Maya and me, as a roommate. It was just for a few days. Maya and I slept in the loft in the back room and she slept on one of the little bed-couches in the front room. Her operation was scheduled for several days later and Maya and I were going to support her through it, drive her there and back. It was now the last snow of the year, February snow again, as we inched up to Courtenay, all three of us, crammed into Selene's much travelled Hillman. We were really only trying to survive the life we had created for ourselves, trying to do something that would work for all three of us, trying to do the right thing.

The young doctor who was going to do the surgery wanted to meet with Selene in his office before the operation. She had heard about him because he was the only doctor willing to be the medical back-up for home births. He had helped many back-to-the-lander babies into the world. If he were a Tarot card he would have been the figure that stood by the small gate by which babies enter the world.

On our way up to Courtenay it began to snow heavily and we realized we would arrive too late for the appointment. We stopped at a gas station and Selene walked through the swirling storm to the payphone. She climbed back into the car, her hair dusted with snowflakes, and said that the doctor still wanted to see her; that he had asked that we meet him in the evening at a restaurant in a part of town that was plowed and easy to get to. It was well after dark when we got there. All three of us went in and the doctor met with all of us. We sat in a booth with him and sipped coffee while he listened to our story. He was supportive and encouraging: he told us he liked how we were all working together. He told Selene that the operation was simple and that most likely what she had was a benign cyst.

We said goodbye to the doctor and went to a nearby motel that was almost empty. All three of us sat in the deserted motel sauna, trying to warm up. Maya led us in chants, and Selene, small, chastened, said she would like to learn more about spirituality and yoga from us. It was strange being in the company of both women.

In the morning Selene got up early and drove her Hillman up the road to the hospital to be prepped. I was to come later, to be there to support her. The very idea of surgery was very frightening to us then. We didn't believe in western medicine and tried to deal with whatever ailed us with herbs and diet.

This is what I remember: hitching up the snowclad road to be there and not being able to get a ride. Why did I assume that I could just stick out my thumb and get a ride? So there I was still standing at the side of the road, which was heaped up with snow banks from the snowploughs. Time was slipping away and I was not there for Selene. I started walking as fast as I could, walking with my thumb out, thinking that maybe I could just walk the five kilometers. The early morning sun reflected off the snowy mountainside, the snow-caked trees, the icy road. Cars clinked slowly by with their chains jingling. I pulled out my grandfather's gold watch—now it sits locked away in a safe-deposit box— and saw that I had failed: the operation was already happening—its time had come—and I had not gotten there in time. I walked quickly along the road slowly chanting Om Mani Padme Hum, the only mantra that I knew, chanting it for Selene's safety, praying she would be alright, that she would not have a malignancy, praying that she would not suffer too much pain.

I wonder how we all could have been so blind. The only answer I can give is that we were all only 22 or 23, living in such a different world from that of our parents (aren't all children, though, a voice inside me says), so disoriented with the drugs that we thought were opening the doors to perception and giving us the insight necessary to evolve. What a mess we made of things. Now I realise why forgiveness plays so prominent a part in religion, particularly self-forgiveness. We all must make amends for the mistakes of living. We were just trying to make lives for ourselves. Om Mani Padme Hum.

So I arrived after it was all over and was led into the recovery room by the compassionate doctor. He told me that Selene's growth was not malignant and that she would still be able to have children if she wanted them. I held Selene's hand and looked into her eyes as she opened and closed them, struggling to find a foothold in consciousness again. I just kept saying, "You are alright now, you're alright," over and over again. When she was fully awake the doctor came in and sat beside her. He sat on the other side of the bed and held her other hand. He looked in her eyes and told her the growth was not malignant and there was no reason she would not be able to have children in the future.

After the doctor left Selene got dressed. They cut off her hospital bracelet and we got into our coats and

208

hats and walked out into the frozen parking lot. She
showed me where she had parked the car. I drove her
down the hill in her little Hillman. We picked up Maya
at the motel, taking some time to pack up our stuff and
headed out on the snowy highway. We stopped for tea
at a little cafe on the outskirts of town. Afterward we
folded ourselves back into Selene's Hillman and went on
our way again.

After that, it is hard to say what happened. Who
was Selene staying with? Where did she go? Gone.

At some point she did come back to the island and
moved in with Russ. But something had happened before
that. Russ and she had a child together and even bought
some land in some remote corner of the island and
began to homestead. Eventually, that did not last either
and she and her daughter moved off the island to a town
across the water.

I did not see her then. I knew little of why this—the
break-up, the moving off the island—had all happened. I
was not a part of her circle anymore. She had lived at
the other end of the island and people did not travel
around much then. People stayed home and worked in
their gardens and on their houses. People stayed home
and cut their wood for winter; visited with their
neighbours, people who were close enough to walk

down the road—or the trail—to visit at the end of the day.

It seemed to me that work became a panacea for us, as it did for Justine in the *Alexandria Quartet*, to deliver us from all the confusion we had created. Fences were built, soil was turned, trees were felled, lumber was milled; proud houses were built where shacks had stood before. The world started again.

I felt strange still living in my little kerosene lighted shack while most of the people I knew had houses of shining new lumber with plate glass windows; had solar panels that illuminated the country night with silent white light. I felt like a second class citizen. I had not moved on. The funny thing is that people with prospering farms and beautiful houses would sometimes confide in me that they envied me the time I still had to walk on the bluffs and to play my flute. Maybe we could have traded: I could have had a nice farm and lots of work to do, and they could have had a shack again and all that time on their hands. Would any of us have been happier?

One day, long after I had moved off Vasquez, when I was visiting a friend in a town near Duncan, I ran into Selene. She and her daughter happened to be visiting the same person. When my friend took Selene's daughter out to the garden to help her hoke out some *potatoes for dinner, Selene and I had a chance to talk. She told me about a man she had met. He had moved to Canada from Poland. Heaven knows how he had gotten into the country. He lived in a plastic shack above one of the great rivers that come crashing down out of Vancouver Island's mountains; that carve deep gorges full of sculpted swimming holes, bright green eyes in the island's stone body.*

She told me that he had lived with the roar of the river for so long that it had washed away his mind, his past, his worries about the future, his habits, his compulsions, all the goals and shoulds that form such a big part of most people's lives. He simply lived by the river and made beautiful little paintings, tiny multi-layered renaissance canvasses full of glowing realism. Each canvas was a small world that could be peered into for a very long time. Aside from this, he lived in the present moment, the moment that was always rushing by like the river itself.

Several years later I met her again and her belly was big with her second child. I had dropped by the house where she lived with her new husband, not the original plastic shack by the river, but a hand-made house they had built on land that they had actually bought. It was not as close to the river as the original shack, but she told me that on clear nights, when the

211

highway noise had died down, you could still hear the sound of the water, mixed with the wind, coming like a whisper through the second growth forest. She had married him. Their house was post and beam, using lots of bent knees, cut and polished from sinuous cedar. It was filled with beautiful old paned windows that they had salvaged from houses that were about to be torn down. She walked me over to a fireplace that they had built from rounded river rock and showed me one of his tiny paintings. "This is when I decided to marry him," she said, "when he gave me this."

I leaned forward and let myself be drawn into the painting. Light shining out from its layer after layer of dark paint drew me in. It was like life itself, shining for its moment out of the darkness before disappearing back into it; it was as if the images in it had just winked on for this moment and would soon wink out again. It showed, illuminated in a garden, a very old couple sitting on a bench. Though wrinkled, wizened and shrunken, they were glowingly happy. They were holding hands and all around them, growing up a trellises, twined morning glories whose blossoms shone out of the dark paint like blue stars. With a jolt I realized that though wrinkled and old they were unmistakably Selene and her husband, sitting together at the end of a long and happy life. "It was in the moment that he gave

212

me this that I decided to marry him and have his child. It all happened in just that moment." With all our plans and goals and striving and patient work we forget how much can happen in a moment.

And so Selene repaired the brokenness of her life, the brokenness of our time and moved on to find a new sanity. I left looking at my own brokenness, wondering about the unrepaired flaw that rumbled through all my relationships.

It was with the intention of being true to my vows of "forever" with Maya that I did not go back to Selene. Maya's and my relationship lasted only a short while after the trip to Courtenay. Apparently you cannot simply decide with somebody to have a relationship that lasts "forever." There must be fate, a certain affinity, an agreement of the unconscious, or of the stars, for that to happen. I heard that Maya had renounced relationship after her time with me and had become a nun in one of the spiritual traditions. Was this about me leaving my stamp on women? Or was it about the women who I picked to try and live a life with?

Selene escaped, Selene with whom I had perhaps one of the most difficult and confusing of runs. She was remarkably resilient, supported by the Tarot and by the great web of astrology in which all our planets hang. She believed in fate and fate did not let her down. Her children have grown up. I heard that one of her daughters got married in a gown woven from flower petals. Selene will always be beautiful, even as an old woman. Her husband saw that and painted it. May they live together until the end of their days.

XVI
The Spatial Location of Time and the Fading of Memory

Around the corner from tomorrow. Kitty-corner from now. Across the street from yesterday. Even as he writes, his time recedes into the distance. Memory fails and the sea of oblivion rises around him, leaving only disconnected peaks, islands of memory, standing above its water.

He sits in his studio, which used to be a wealthy lady's walk-in closet—he is truly a closet writer. He examines each of these islands, looks at the signs in the dirt, the foundation stones, the few things that he remembers that really happened, and catalogues them. He knows from the trade beads that such and such an event was connected to events over on that other island, the one he can see across a short stretch of water. But the sea has risen.

He looks to where his canoe is pulled up on the beach, to see if it needs to be pulled even higher so the rising tide won't float it away. He cannot quite remember how the islands connect: the trails between them are covered with rising Lethe, with eternity now. It sounds like a political slogan to him: "Eternity Now!" He can see a crowd of angry protesters raising their fists and chanting it on the parliament lawns.

He remembers those trails, the well-packed paths of damp soil that passed through old alders whose white trunks rose like columns from the forest floor; that passed through arching salmonberry, whose blossoms were violet flames in spring, whose berries were faceted gems in summer. Gone forever beneath the sea.

He will have to paddle out to that other island, the one that's over there, to see if he can remember exactly what happened. Or maybe he will have to make it up, create something that feels right, something that would fit, like a palaeontologist putting a face and a personality on a skull: in his hands it becomes a smiling young woman dressed in furs, holding out a bouquet of yellow flowers to welcome the returning hunters.

Ah yes, the skulls that once sang and danced, told stories, stored memories and did a thousand foolish and wonderful things before they became artifacts, empty seashells that fell to the bottom of the sea. So many of his friends who lived through this time are dead; so many of those who remain don't have many years left. Each remembers fragments.

Sometimes, on one of those islands of memory, he finds an old house. There is a picture of a person in it, left tacked on a wall or buried in a pile of leaves and old boards. Who were they? He remembers a few things. He rummages through his memory as though it were one of the jumbled boxes in the Vasquez Island Free Store. Sometimes he finds a shirt that he remembers someone having worn. He holds it up in the darkness of the store and says out loud, "if you see yourself in this book, fear not, it is not really you, it's just one of my characters dressed up in some of the old clothes you threw away."

Even as he ponders all this, the sea is rising. He hears the waves beginning to bang against the canoe. He looks over his shoulder to make sure it isn't being floated off the beach, that it doesn't need to be pulled still higher. His old body aches. It's easy for his back to go out. He is a far cry from the inflamed youths he is writing about.

Outside his studio it is early morning. A new day is dawning with new papers to read. New land is rising. Yesterday at the beach he saw a man lift a woman onto a log and then lift her blouse and kiss her breasts. He imagines the feeling of passion that must have been surging through them on that sunny afternoon. Lichens and the grasses colonise the new land. New creatures

217

emerge. He could be enjoying all this, working in his garden, weeding his Echinaca or planting a new bed of lettuce, but instead he writes, trying to capture some of this and string it together before it becomes isolated, fragmented memories. It is a gift to his children; to the remaining ones with whom he lived through this time; to people in the future who might wonder what those long haired back-to-the-landers were all about, aside from the cartoons in the newspapers.

He has been struck, inflicted, wounded with the knowledge that he is disappearing along with all life forms, along with their memories, along with their time. What remains of all this struggle, he wonders. What will be transported, as the seas rise, to the new land? What is worth keeping from this marvellous and tragic procession called life?

XVII
Standing On The Wharf

Standing on the wharf after a rare trip back to Vasquez, Ryan realises that much of what he has written about has already vanished. Many of the people who lived on Vasquez during his time have already died or moved away. He looks around. Only a few stragglers are still carrying things from the ferry to their cars. Ryan takes one last look around and then walks to his car to start the long drive home.

In Anne Lamott's book, *All New People*, a father and his young daughter are standing on the shores of San Francisco Bay. As they look out at the sprawling megalopolis, he says to her, with a sweep of his hand, "In a hundred years all new people will live here."

It will only be in about twenty years that all new people from the ones that Ryan knew will live on Vasquez. Even today, he noticed that the ferry was full of fresh young faces. He wondered about their experience. Did they grow gardens? Did they do drugs?

Were their relationships more or less stable than his had been? Were they in rebellion? Did they fear for the continuance of the world? Did they dream of a different world? Did they raise their children not to have the same limitations that had been imposed on them?

While on Vasquez, Ryan had visited an old friend, also in his seventies and who had just ended a long relationship with his wife. His friend's house was a hand-built back-to-the-lander house with all the requisite curves, garrets and bay windows of the time. It used to be so elegant but now was beginning to look old. The shakes were grey and had tufts of moss and lichen growing on them. Ryan saw a bit of rot in the footings at the bottom of the stairs. Things needed to be replaced. Inside were the work benches, the photographs, the artwork, the crystals collected over a lifetime. It was the house of an old man.

On the ferry back, Ryan had seen Skip, a man who used to live on Vasquez when he did. Ryan had been in his forties then, with the first streaks of grey in his hair; Skip was just a young man. Now Skip was married to an island woman and himself had streaks of grey; Ryan's hair—what was left of it—had gone completely white.

Ryan asked him so many questions, "Whatever happened to..." and Skip told him the story of many of people and places that Ryan had not seen since he lived there. Skip told him that the old log house, the one in which Ryan had said goodbye to Selene, had burned down.

"It was bought and fixed up by someone, really nice, they'd put in windows, and then it burnt down. No one has been there for a long time and the fields are growing up in alders."

"How 'bout the orchard?"

Skip told him that the fruit trees that Ryan, Stewart, Curtis and Mark had played Frisbee among on that day that Ryan had walked up to the mountain, were now swallowed by the forest.

"You probably wouldn't even recognise the place anymore."

The forest was erasing it all, taking back all the little stages upon which Ryan had played his part in the little human dramas that he had written about.

Skip also told him that Mike, the scary old caretaker, was dead, "Taken off to Vancouver to die."

Ryan asked him what had become of Mike's wild land; of the great old trees that he'd preserved; of the two houses that were already rotting in Ryan's time, the one up at the homestead and the one down by the beach; of the fences that Mike had laboured to keep from falling down. Skip said, "I don't know, the houses have probably been looted by now."

"Did he leave it to anyone," Ryan asked, "did he have any heirs?"

"I don't know, I haven't heard anything. He was the seventh son of a seventh son, you know."

"Does that mean that he was the end of his line, that there was no-one after him?"

"I don't know."

Later Ryan learned that Mike had left his land to a charity for homeless children, no doubt envisioning happy orphans running up and down his beach, shouting and playing in the sand. The charity then sold it to the CEO of one of the great American banks. He then bulldozed the houses, built tennis courts and created a great gated estate—NO TRESPASSING.

But the land was still there. In his mind's eye Ryan saw the great crescent of Mike's beach unencumbered by human life at last. It reminded him of the Robinson Jeffers' poem, *Carmel Point*:

The extraordinary patience of things!
This beautiful place defaced with a crop of suburban
    houses—
How beautiful when we first beheld it,
Unbroken field of poppy and lupin walled with clean
    cliffs;

No intrusion but two or three horses pasturing,
Or a few milch cows rubbing their flanks on the outcrop
rockheads—
Now the spoiler has come: does it care?
Not faintly. It has all time. It knows the people are a tide
That swells and in time will ebb, and all
Their works dissolve. Meanwhile the image of the pris-
tine beauty
Lives in the very grain of the granite,
Safe as the endless ocean that climbs our cliff. —As for
us:
We must uncenter our minds from ourselves;
We must unhumanize our views a little, and become
confident
As the rock and the ocean that we were made from.

Ryan had also seen a matronly woman on the boat. At first he thought she was one of the old timers who was already there when he first came to Vasquez. Then he realised that she couldn't be: that she would have to be much older now, or maybe even dead. Skip said that she was the child of the woman that Ryan was remembering, a look-alike daughter who had now become an old-timer herself. Ryan remembered her name when it was spoken, and her long dark hair from

223

long ago, and her aloofness from the hippies on the boat. Now she looked exactly like her mother.

Ryan walks away from the silent ferry, up the ramp to his car, to start the long drive back to to Sooke and his own time. He winds past Nanoose with all its stories and submarines. Even though it is longer, he takes the old highway that goes through the long strip malls of Nanaimo. They are still there. He even takes a little detour and drives down Nanaimo's winding main street. There are a thousand experiences at different places along this road and it's reassuring to him that somewhere off the freeway there are still some pieces left of the world in which he used to live.

At the town of Malahat, which is really just a post office, gas station and restaurant tucked into a widening curve of the road, he drives up a dirt road to a junkyard called Malahat Motors. He has come to get something called a Beauty Ring—a piece of decorative trim that fits inside one of the wheels of his Jetta. He has been refurbishing the car after writing in the morning, well ok, sometimes before writing, waxing it and repairing missing pieces of trim so that it looks shinier and more up to date than it really is. He thinks it's harder on Cora than it is on him that they drive an older car: it's not that they are poor; they have a house, or a mortgage, in one of the better parts of town. It's just that they are out-classed, surrounded by doctors and lawyers who they imagine are curious about how they manage to live there. He finds refurbishing the car much more concrete and satisfying than writing. He really should be hiring someone else to do the dirty work with the car; in reality, he should have a newer car that doesn't require dirty work. But, truth be known, he still likes the tinkering with old machines that was so much a part of his life on Vasquez.

So every now and then, in a space that isn't scheduled, he buggers off to track down some part that he refuses to pay full price for at the Volkswagen dealer. It's bad enough that they charge $3.95 for a small plastic stud that holds a piece of trim on the door. Just imagine what a Beauty Ring must cost.

He bounces over the ruts as he drives through a forest of young pines and firs and parks next to the bright blue cinder block office. Inside, under the fluorescent lights, a young man is furiously wrapping an engine in plastic, preparing it to be shipped. He is black haired, wears a blue T-shirt, and is covered with tattoos.

"Can I help you?"

"Yeah, I called a few days ago about a Beauty Ring for a Jetta."

He is embarrassed to use the words "Beauty Ring." Is that really what they are called or was it just a joke by some guy in one of the parts houses? To his surprise the words work. It is always nice when the words work.

"Yeah, go up there, just past the bend in the road. You'll see some Jettas. One just come in a few days ago with some Beauty Rings on it. Pull off the one you want."

Ryan goes back to his car to get the large screw driver and the vice grips that he has brought. He walks up the hill in the direction the tattooed man has pointed. The entire junkyard fits into several acres of clearing the way a pond might fit into a fold of the forest. It is truly beautiful here: above the steep hillside there is a ridge of fir trees. In the tops of the trees crows sit cawing. Below him a dark curve of Finlayson arm is visible just below a bend in the Island Highway.

The whole area is covered by rows and rows of cars in various stages of disassembly and disintegration: hoods are gone, engines are gone, wheels are gone, trunk lids are gone. Gone, Gone Beyond, Gone Beyond the Beyond. It reminds him of his Buddhist mechanic who got his vows screwed up and dedicated his life to saving all old Datsuns and Toyotas, no matter how innumerable. Some of the cars are propped up on stacks of metal wheels so that people can crawl around underneath to pull off parts. Grass grows between and around the cars. The ground is littered with parts and shattered glass. It is an industrial killing field, a cemetery for old cars that have served their purpose and now are only good for a few more parts to keep the living alive.

He loves the junkyard. He finds in it a huge metaphor for the end of civilisation out among the crows and blackberries. Surely this civilisation must end someday? Babylon did. The great Indian kingdoms did. Athens did. Rome did. The Chinese dynasties did. Even bees and educated flees do it.

Cultural collapse: accepting death, living inside the end of things, living for today and not forever. Why should we think, he wonders, that we will go brightly on forever, especially when so many clouds of doom gather in the sky around us like Mongol hoards.

The junkyard is also a metaphor for the various sub-lives he has led: abandoned occupations, relationships, homes, communities, friends that he still carries parts of around inside himself, out of which he still operates: like Sheila showing him how to put a bedspread on symmetrically, how to line up the pattern with the square of the mattress; like his love and competence for keeping old machinery running that he learned on Vasquez; like his ability to mop floors that he learned as a conscientious objector in the corridors of Sacred Heart hospital; like Selene showing him how to read Tarot or Maya teaching him about Zen meditation.

He looks all over and cannot find the beauty rings. They all seem to have been stripped from the wheels of the derelict Jettas. It is like an automotive skid row up here, full of cars that can't function any more, that sell a pint of blood here, a hub cap there, an alternator tomorrow, all to hold the crusher at bay for one more day.

He comes down and talks to the black haired man who is still wrapping tape, spools and spools of tape, around the plastic cocoon.

"I must be missing something but I didn't see any beauty rings up there."

"I'll run up and have a look."

He puts down his tape and takes off up the hill at a full-tilt run. Ryan runs after him. Why is he in such a hurry? Ryan struggles to keep up; his floppy Birkenstocks keep falling off his feet.

At the top of the hill, behind the Jettas that Ryan had looked at, behind the corpses of several rusting old Saabs—the junk yard must be arranged by geographical region—the young man points to yet another Jetta that Ryan hadn't seen.

"It just come in a couple of days ago. I think it's got three rings on it. Take which one you want."

Then he runs fleetly back down the hill to return to his cocoon building. Ryan realises that he must be rushing to get the engine out with a courier that he's already called.

Ryan uses his screwdriver to pry off the rings. He looks at each of them. None of them are perfect. Each of them is missing some of the spring-tabs that hold them on the wheel. He picks the one that looks the best and walks down the hill and snaps it on his Jetta. While not exactly right, it does stay on the car. He steps back. The car looks complete, waxed, shiny, its trim all in place. Looking at it no one would know about all of the parts and pieces that came from the lives of other cars.

He pays the eight dollars plus PST and GST and drives back to his present time, back to his home, to his wife. He is quite glad to come back to this saner version of himself, to simply be an old man with the fire and confusion of youth behind him. There is always time for love, even love for his former self, the young man who landed him where he is today, which, he has to admit, despite the pile of regrets on the empty seat beside him, is not so bad. One of the *Cold Mountain Poems* comes to mind:

In my first thirty years of life
I roamed hundreds and thousands of miles.
Walked by rivers through deep green grass
Entered cities of boiling red dust.
Tried drugs, but couldn't make Immortal;
Read boos and wrote poems on history.
Today I'm back at Cold Mountain:
I'll sleep by the creek and purify my ears.

When he arrives home, the sun is down behind the trees but it is still light. Only a few high clouds still have the sunlight of this day upon them. He carries his pack in the door and is welcomed back by Cora who comes out of the kitchen to greet him. She is glad to have him back home after his weekend away. She hugs him and he luxuriates for a moment in that most amazing thing, the deep love of another person.

With each visit to Vasquez the haunting becomes less: more and more it becomes just a place where he used to live.

XVIII
Selene

A southeast storm, rain mixed with hail and wet snow, rushes up out of Washington state. As the front hits Vancouver, huge gusts buffet the high-rises, while out on the street people run for cover.

In a warehouse in Yaletown, Indian Jim stands over his son who is carving the eyes of a huge totem that lies on its back like a fallen hero. On its stand, its blank unfinished eyes appear to be gazing upwards at the steel girders and gritty skylight. Jim's hair is still fine but now it is mostly grey with just a few strands of black. He stands next to his son, a muscular teenage boy with the fine hair of his father, except that it is cut short and gelled into short spikes that look like the crest of a bird. He holds the bright chisel and wooden mallet in his hand, cutting away the space around the pupil of the totem's left eye. Jim leans over him and occasionally passes his finger over the texture of the wood. Besides them, on a small school chair, sits a little girl who is also carving, a small piece of cedar that she holds on her lap.

She has carved a small, potato-like, likeness of Jim. When she shows it to him he laughs. "Yeah, it kinda looks like me," he says. She uses her little chisel skilfully, swiftly taking away what is not him, leaving rudimentary features, eyes, nose, mouth, to denote her father. Jim does not worry about her cutting herself. They have been through that already.

When the storm hits, they all look up at the skylight for a moment. A gust of wind strikes the building and hail stones ping off the skylight's glass. Jim walks over and looks out the window. "Storm's here," he says softly. Even across the street the buildings are fading into invisibility, erased by the thickening snow and hail, erased by the gathering darkness.

The storm continues over Vancouver and breaks like a wave on the North Shore mountains. It continues up Georgia Strait lashing the waves into foam; spattering the sea with rain and hail. The grey-blue world of evening fades into nothing as the storm turns itself to snow.

The storm is too big for the basin of the Gulf of Georgia, and overflows into the mountains of Vancouver Island, raging into the Albernie pass, howling, trying to find its way to the freedom of the west coast. On its way, it knocks down some of the old-growth trees in

Cathedral Grove, a pathetic little stand of virgin forest that the logging company has begrudgingly left in order to tout itself as a good corporate citizen. The grove is surrounded by broken mountains covered with nothing but stumps and fireweed. A woman, driving east through the Albernie Pass, is passing through the grove. Her hair is grey; her face is tanned and is lined with laughter and sorrow. She is wearing a smart green dress that is embroidered with a Plains Indian bead motif. A small obsidian arrowhead hangs on a silver chain around her neck. She brakes at the first snowflakes, turns on her lights, her defroster, and her windshield wipers. She continues to drive, but much more slowly.

The grove is alive with winds. As the woman drives through it, her face contracts. In a mock preacher's voice, to entertain herself, she says out loud, shouting over the CBC, gesticulating with one hand, "Yeah, smoke and soot shall fill thy cities; thy seas shall be clogged with filth; even thy mountains shall be laid waste. Naught but nettles and brambles shall grow where once mighty forests stood." Then she laughs but her eyes are filled with tears. The woman is Selene.

She continues east in the fading light, trying to get home to Duncan before dark, before the brunt of the storm hits. She is returning from a tedious meeting in Ucluelet where she had given expert testimony to document a native land claim. Rather than become upset by the absurdities of these meetings, the acrimony, the struggle by the government not to give anything away, she has learned how to usually laugh her way through them. She is glad that her skills, learned so long ago in university, can be put to some good use. "Well, look at it this way: we took away their land, their religion, their children; we abused their children. We took away their ritual implements—how would we feel if someone came into our churches and took away all the crosses and statues of saints? We enslaved them to work in our coal mines. We shelled their villages. We gave them syphilis and small pox. Don't you think, after all that, that it's reasonable for them to ask that this land be given back, and that they be given the right to manage it in their own way? My report shows that this land has clearly, evidentially, been used by them for thousands of years before we even came. They are not taking it away from us. We took it away from them."

She hadn't said this angrily, vehemently. She had said it in a voice full of laughter, like she could barely keep a straight face at the absurdity of anyone wanting to deny the claim. She knows that the Indian Affairs people were upset with her for saying this. Her place was just to present the evidence, neutrally, without comment.

But she had been pissed off and really didn't care. The representatives from Indian Affairs had come to the meeting an hour late, by helicopter. They had arrived while an elder was speaking. He had long grey hair and was wearing an embroidered ceremonial robe of red and black. On his head was a square wooden hat with the carved face of an owl on the front. He was talking about his father's relationship to the land, his grandfather's relationship to the land, his great grandfather's relationship to the land. Even further back, he had known exactly when the first humans—his people—had come here, and from where. All this had survived in the oral tradition, even despite the smallpox. Selene's job had been to substantiate it.

As the elder talked, the sound of the helicopter had become progressively louder. The great thup thup thup of its rotors and roar of its engine had drowned out his soft voice. The school room shook with its vibrations. Finally, the Elder stopped speaking, his words, and his thoughts, drowned out by this great machine descending from the sky. The whole meeting just stopped and they all watched through the big windows of the classroom as the helicopter lowered itself into the school yard. Two white men dressed in suits got out. They stooped low to avoid the big rotors that were still swirling above their heads. With one hand, they held their hats, with the other they clutched great brief cases that looked stuffed with paper.

"Department of Indian Affairs," someone said in a soft native accent. There was gentle laughter in the room. Once past the rotors, the two men straightened up and arranged their coats and ties. They walked straight into the school, through the door to the class room, and then straight up to the podium at the front of the room. They seemed to be unaware that a speech was already in progress. The elder stepped aside. He took off his ceremonial hat and sat quietly back down in the front row. One of the Indian Affairs officials took the podium. He looked around for a place to put his hat and found some chairs at the back of the platform. The other bureaucrat sat next to the hat.

The speaker smiled beefily at his audience. "Sure is great to be here today." Outside the windows, the rotors of the helicopter were coasting slowly to a stop. The pilot had stepped out and was lighting up a smoke. He walked around the school yard, puffing away, stopping to look at some totems and a canoe that were on display out under a large shaked roof. The bureaucrat took some papers out of his rain spattered briefcase and read a complicated position paper from the federal government, about the policy ramifications of aboriginal self-government. It was full of comments about levels of government, competing levels of government, sovereignty, provincial rights, municipal rights, federal rights. It was as obfuscating and noncommittal as anything could be: King Solomon making hamburger from a disputed child could not have minced things more finely. Words, words, words. Words upon words. When he was finished the other representative got up and asked for questions. He must have been the lawyer who could interpret all this. He seemed quite surprised when there were none. He and the other man were starting to pack up, starting to move to the back of the room, when Selene got up. That was when she delivered her little tirade.

The two men exchanged glances. She had clearly ruffled them. The lawyer said "We all wish it could be just as simple as that." They walked to the back of the room and took seats under the children's poster paintings, paintings that depicted raven releasing people from a clam shell; that depicted Sisiuitle talking with his two heads; that depicted people battling sea monsters in fragile canoes. There was silence in the room. The elder shuffled back to the podium, put on his hat and continued his speech. "As I was saying," he said. His voice was soft, and even from the back of the room they could see the flash of his gold teeth.

Selene remembers all this as she drives past Cameron Lake and down the long slope that drops to the Gulf of Georgia. When she reaches the place where you can see the sea for the first time, the sky lifts for just a minute. Out across the stormy waters she catches a glimpse of Vasquez, the place where once, so long ago, she had lived; where once upon a time, so much or so little—depending on how she looked at it—happened. Now it was just an island, a dark forested spot swept by rain and snow out among the waves. She wipes condensation from the driver's side window and strains to see the island, but it appears only for a moment and then the sky closes around it; the wind and sleety rain completely erasing it from view, hiding everything that was once visible. Selene turns to face the road ahead. She, clicks on her signal and slows to negotiate the on-ramp. She checks her watch and speeds up a bit as she changes lanes and enters the great highway that will take her home.

Acknowledgements:

I would like to extend thanks to: early readers Susan and Laurie Geddes, Laura Anderson, Doug MacDonald, Lhasa Hetherington and Peggy Hansen. Special thanks to Doug for his thoughtful suggestions. Thanks to Ann Eriksson for her comments—difficult to hear at the time—without which this book would not have been born. Thanks to later readers Helen Porter, Yarrow Drake, Bruce Johnson, Tolling Jennings, and Kay Meierbachtol. Thanks to Dan Rubin for being (among other things) a font of helpful ideas and showing me some editing paradigms. To Peggy Hansen and Susan Breiddal for help with descriptions of the book and many hours of patient editing: all remaining errors are obstinately mine alone. To Lhasa Hetherington for title ideas, help with the description of the book, cover design and navigating the digital world. To Nicola Furlong for her excellent course on online publishing. To Fran Aitkens for help with designing the print version. The quotes from the I-Ching in chapters 11 and 12 are from *The I Ching Or Book of Changes,* Hellmut Wilhelm, editor. Translated by Cary F. Baynes. Copyright © 1950, 1967 Bollingen Foundation Inc. Reproduced by permission of Princeton University Press. The poem in chapter 17, "Carmel Point," is copyright © 1954 by

Robinson Jeffers and renewed 1982 by Donnan Call Jeffers & Garth Jeffers; from *THE SELECTED POETRY OF ROBINSON JEFFERS* by Robinson Jeffers. Used by permission of Random House, an imprint and division of Penguin Random House LLC. All rights reserved. The Cold Mountain Poem by Han Shan also in chapter 17 is Copyright © 2009, from *Rip Rap and Cold Mountain Poems,* by Gary Snyder. Reprinted by permission of Counterpoint (though I first discovered it hand-written and tacked to the wall of a cabin on one of the Gulf Islands). Thanks to Gabriella Onderwyzer, Manfred Wolfe, and Ray Rice for recognising my writing ability and, each in their own way, encouraging me to continue. Most importantly, thanks to my wife Peggy Hansen for her support during the years of writing this.

About the Author

In his misspent youth, Arnold W. Porter lived as a back to the lander on one of the Gulf Islands in British Columbia. In writing *In a Time of Magic*, he has drawn on his degree in literature from San Francisco State University, his interest in Taoism and eastern religions, his master's degree in counselling from the University of Victoria, and an understanding of human nature developed through 35 years as a counsellor. He currently lives with his wife in Victoria, BC where he writes, plays music, practices yoga and tai chi, and works as a hospice counsellor.